Wilderness House Literary Review

edited by Gloria Mindock

The best of Volume 1 (2006)

www.iscspress.com
145 Foster Street
Littleton MA 01460 USA

www.lulu.com/

ISBN 978-0-6151-6265-2

This book was designed by Steve Glines
Headline fonts are Tempus Sans ITC
Body type is Palatino Linotype

Wilderness House Literary Review

The best of Volume 1 (2006)

The Bagel Bards in the summer of 2007

Forward

The *Wilderness House Literary Review* began as a result of the collaboration between a group of poets and writers who call themselves the "Bagel Bards" and the *Wilderness House Literary Retreat*. The retreat lent its name to the review.

The "Bagel Bards" are a remarkable collection of very talented editors, writers and poets. Without their talent and time neither the WHLReview nor this anthology would exist.

- Our poetry editor, Irene Koronas, is not only a talented and award winning experimental poet, she is also the artist who painted our cover.

- Doug Holder, our book review editor, is one of the most prolific writers I have ever met. My electronic in-box is pleasantly filled every day by the output of his creative hand. Doug Holder together with Harris Gardner are the godparents of the "Bagel Bards" having assembled the group from among their literary acquaintances.

- Our fiction editor, Julia Carlson, has the unenviable task of wading through tons of stuff she says is "not Chekhov." A poem can be read in fifteen or twenty seconds but sifting through hundreds of not-so-short stories takes dedication.

Finally in addition to thanking the scribes who's work fills this book I'd like to thank Gloria Mindock of Červená Barva Press who took on the task of winnowing down a years worth of WHLreview to produce what I consider to be an exceptional work of literature.

Steve Glines,
editor, Wilderness House Literary Review

John Martin, The Bard, 1817
Laing Art Gallery, Newcastle-upon-Tyne, England

Contents

The art of Irene Koronas

Autodidact

I will let go of everything I've learned.
With time comes, not really wisdom,
but a recognition of repeated patterns.
My memories meander in;
we watch the sunset over the lake,
or wake in the night mesmerized by moonlight.
It is the moment that matters most to me,
like the flash of fireflies that burst into view
and disappear into the dark.

- Lainie Senechal

Return from the Cove

I round the bend
in retreat from the cove.
A strong pull on the left paddle
to make the turn
and face a moon half full.
She has already begun a serenade
to the surface of the lake,
striking a thousand keys
with sparks from flashing fingers.
The Naiads notice each note;
they reply with a reedy refrain.
For me it is a silent song
from the beginnings of moon
   and lake.
I reach into the dark waters
to anoint myself with the sound
of liquid and light.

- Lainie Senechal

FICTIONS

You will love me forever, until you became
bored with predictability and leave me
for a man who plays board games and
grows the best pot you ever smoked

After being beaten
my belief in mother love falters
only eleven years old
and exhausted by her love

I simply forgive

Even animals must flee when frightened

Falling out of mind
into life
they are orphans
Mysteries of mind leaving me silent

as I await further direction

- Charles P. Ries

IDEAS OF GRACE

Moments of desolation when life and love collide
drowning us beneath the weight of their inevitability
You pause and look back at me as if I were cancer
How can this be?

Why is this happening?

Who do you think you are?

Isn't history the antidote for bad judgment?

Fidelity is so fluid these days
So much expected in return

I tell you about my parents
My long suffering mother
My long silent father
Married 58 years until death
"Those were days of denial, when relationship
 was abduction and silence a woman's ransom."

I don't argue   I hide my point of view

How could you understand
there is glory in surrender
if made for harmony

Or that the liberation of the blind
 is conceived in a bed of forgiveness

- Charles P. Ries

Love

Love always comes
disassembled.

You have to put it
softly together

piece by quiet piece
until love appears

much better than that
imagined before.

- Robin Dancer

Reverence

  I worship my deities from the pew
of a scrambled alphabet. I type
my prayers to silent old women in black
squeezing cantaloupes in vegetable stands.

  No grace speaks louder than the tongue
of a mute boy. Together, we work
in the fields in the sun, use the virtue
of our hands to quench thirst, twisting
fingers for the perfect iced tea.

  There is not enough piety in metal idols
to know when fruit is ripe, the quantity
of sugar required. The bread is too thin
to sustain, wine dispersed in drops.

  When I walk, I walk slowly to see gods.
When I pray, I pray softly. My ears
are close by. So are my fingertips.

(first appeared in The Pedestal Magazine)

- Patrick Carrington

BUTTERFLIES

These ugly worms weave
Their caskets from brown spit.
Threads of saliva
Are wrapped like watery vines
Around their tombs.

Butterflies are the best proof
For resurrection.
They are not nailed to the cross
By their own, and still.
They rise and fly to glory.

Unashamed of its desire for isolation,
The worm seeks out
A hidden limb
A crevice in the wall
A hole in a fence post.

Hidden throughout winter
Baptized by the rains of spring
They open soggy blood-drenched wings
All over the world.
I would kiss them if I could.

- Julia Carlson

Photo by Steve Glines

ORANGE ON BURNT SIENNA

Cézanne, I cared nothing
for geometry. I learned I loved
you for the wrong reasons.
Only later did I study
your curmudgeonly planes,
your fractured composition,
the range of your influence.
These two card players sit
facing one another
as they have so many times,
laying their cards
on the table. They know
one another's hands.
The brown and yellow
ochre of their coats
and crumpled hats, the white clay pipe—
what life isn't a mess
of coffee stains, tobacco, and sawdust?
You've painted the quiet of an afternoon

- Richard Wilhelm

AS WE LAY SLEEPING

In dream time I was a tailor
and you were a flower girl.
Sometimes you dressed like a gypsy.
Sometimes I wore a gray suit.
In my attic were electric
guitars of many colors:
blue, orange, black, red, purple, green.
One by one I played them while
you held a mirror to the moon.

- Richard Wilhelm

Mend

What whole could I make
if I collected all the shell
fragments on the beach
and pinned them together?
Where would I arrive if
I followed all the footprints?
Refletch the feathers
fallen to each bird.
Spin sand to stone
and back again.
I am your hands.
Electrify my heart
to silent occupation.
Still.

- Kelley J. White

reconfigured

By stevenallenmay

Undulated angular
hell blue half close pale skin
brown eyes, cheeks, her's
primary colors
zigzag streak of green undertone
at chin
as in background vista

Laurel branch
sprig emblematic blonde
intellect and virtue
twines around her confident pose.

Delicate of color and shading
red dots
silkscreened
as rain down from
a same sun
painted small square image.

Meticulous wave locks along snaky texture scales
right side of her head distract from
purple string in bust
blue breast of sky
cloud nipples of desire

Steel nerves Monolith slab
only some last step of stairs
corner red and black wall
--massive gravity sealant
without reason a brute fact

fell to ground floor
in the Hall of Witness.
He wore his
French style draperies in their wanton fullness
Right elbow leans lightly on book column
slender fingers,
left wrist bowed to hip
to behind
as in dance. Hairs bound in long tail
decorated by thread-tied necks
of orthodox priests,

Some details may defy description : full-length
lifelike pine
three folds of skin divide
horizontal chin as mask (off or
on), are almost torn to
indistinguishably near jaw pleats
immediately below the knee,

Horrifyingly gothic elements show
man turning into wood like stoney
furrows; a skeleton for skin and organs
collapsing into immortality.

Apparently reflective
glass-eyes look forward
as far as root growing from the tree
and bottom of neck is drawn
backwards as surplus in defect of physics
as compensated as rich men in breadlines

One foot standing
transformed into a piece
of real rock where pillar is boulder
and ambiguity is a hard act to follow.

Matter fuses to theme, to detail
to surreal genius

in shiny sculpture in back
in its raised arms

Head constrained
too human features
the beholder as
mass different probably human though tail
might one thermomorphous
naive enlargement MirÛ, bare dust

Abrupt reconfiguration
brushes rust to brown
marble chisels into mounds of snow
novels unwrite themselves
Genie swallows the bottle, Jonah
consumes the whale;
all that remains is Ken's body
with Barbie's head
mismatched metaphors for life
as told to a 5 year old
not wanting to sleep.

(poem from his book, 'frac tur ede velo pment' (Plan B
Press))

§

EROS -- Post-Modern.

"All night long massaging our feet with sandlewood oil, a cloudless,
billion-starred sky, full moon and your feet...":

"Moi aussi, la même chose...mais nous sommes separés pour siecles et les
espaces celéstes/ me too, the same thing...but we've been separated by centuries
and celestial spaces..."

Gypsy-her stepping out of the ancient photos all over my walls, just one of
her the way she is now at 92, the eyes still the same.

Gitane-Gypsy cornhusks and tequila, submerging back to sane-times,
before the Aryans come in.
Abrazos,

- Hugh Fox

DOG DANCE

I see your skull veiled by a cloud
Eyelids sunk
Hands pressed on knees
Heart gone
A sight of secrets

In the distance, a dog is howling as the
sirens pass
Does this dog know what I don't?
Is he crying for the dead?

The dead are a miracle
In the cemetery, graves connect and a festival
of arms try to touch one another
Passerby's wave good-bye and the stone
reminds me of their daily labor (of how strong or
brave they were)

I think living is brave
Death is a release
The dog knows--heaven is nothing but a frill

- Gloria Mindock

Momentum

The journey of a thousand miles
Single steps across the land
Following in footsteps
Falling in quicksand

Is meaning in the being,
Or the doing? Or the done?
Is it in a day's work
Or the setting of the sun?

When the ants fight the termites
For a hole or a hill
Would the world be better
If the bugs stood still?
Finally at
The end of violence
The earth turns on its axis
Silence

- Matthew Silver Rosenthal

The art of Deborah Priestly

Four cool cats
(the end of hip and the death of cool)

By Steve Glines

Four cool cats
and one very hip chick
Were ready
to smoke the joint.

The drummer man
began to beat the
Tom tom, ta-ta, tom, tom.
Tom, tom, ta-ta, tom, tom.

His timpani went
Boom boom bim bim, boom boom
Boom boom bim bim, boom boom

rata tat tat tat,
he said on the rims and
brama bumb bum on the snare

Man that cat was cool.
that junky drummer
got every foot
grooving to the beat.

And just
when you didn't know
where else he could take you
with the beat
Mr. Sax crawled in with a
bawha dip

ba du bi da
wahhhha

Just about then I heard
No, felt
the base
dum dum dum dum de
and Ivory man came in with a
de dele de le de le do

man ....
they were smoking up that joint
every cool cat was grooving ...
Then it got quiet

Ivory put his hands in the air
So did drums and Mr. Sax.
But the base said
Ba dum dum dum da dum dum dum

From out of the shadows
One very cool kitten
came into the light
Oh my, she had pipes

She was singing the blues
With her soul
And her heart
And her mind
But she didn't have the blues
Nobody does
cause the blues was dead
Drowned in Nawleanes

I was thinking about that
But she kept pulling me back in
In my head and in the music
Man what a grove.

But the blues was dead
Ashes scattered,
some went to Jazz in Chicago
some went to sleep in Nashville
and some went to rock and roll
but the blues was dead.

I was shedding a tear for the blues
when Mr. Sax wiped his brow
and an old man came out of the shadow
and a toothless grin
from the junky drummer
said that cool was dead
it was the end of hip

This was the last party
The last jam
And the joint was smoking
And the rap man said
Step aside old man
And I knew
it was the end of hip
and the death of cool.

§

Ruins

on the outskirts of you,
tangled in verbal ivy
i harden my tongue,
needing the oration of a blade,
one that slashes
through creepers and stranglers,
and the toys you left here,
now garrisons for slow ants.

i'm guarded by worms,
swallowed by vines,
pinned to the rusty knees of fences.
i stare through hatchets of shadow
at stars that mock what once knew flight.

figs molder near my prostrate thirst.
tangerines nudge with wizened frowns.
everything here is senile, mumbling in mildew,
while i slowly embrace the humus.

- Chris Crittenden

FIRST NAMES

By Carolyn Gregory

How tenuous his voice sounds
when he calls, leaving a first name
and the desire to hear from her.
He's living in San Francisco.
It's fair enough to phone once a decade.

She scratches her head after a long workday
because it's really been twenty years.
For months, she wondered where he was.
No Internet or business linked them,
just the shared sorrow of youth misplaced.

The wedding had been a miracle in the snow,
slipping down slopes in a purple velvet dress
and hand-me-downs.
She thought she knew what love meant.

Two coasts and twenty years apart,
she calls him back to find he's divorced again
with two children and lots of debt.
She confides she's been sad, too,
though she's written serious poetry.

His voice moves far away.
He still polishes his rocket in the yard

to leave the planet eventually
though shadows lie longer in the streets.

Signing off, there's an agreement
to exchange e-mails and snail mails,
discussion of which parents died
and how pride interfered with love

like the vortices of depression,
fueled in the long Michigan winters
they shared when they were young.

§

A Tree of Cats

While my cat was in her impassioned mood
I had a dream of suitors, within a tree of cats
long haired, short haired, black, white and gray
each branch shivered as it beckoned with cat
A prayer moaned the length of the wind
and echoed throughout the listening sky,
each cat so tangled in its maze of unrest
one swung from its long black tail,
another sat calm in the crux of a tree,
while a tabby wiggled its song into the grass
there was no telling how long each cat had stayed
or how long each had sung its longing cry,
but the roots of this tree hug the earth so deep
if one cat did not find love, I would be surprised.

- Deborah Priestly

THE QUIET ROOM

By Doug Holder

My name is Leon...Leon Dunn. Most nights I wake up at 8 or so, still feeling bloated from dinner. Mostly I have early dinners. Eating makes me sleep. I have to sleep...I work nights. I go to school at night. For that matter...most of my days are in the dead of night.

Did I mention that I am 35? I guess I'm young to some, not so young to others. I live in a room. The room is quite small. It's a walk-up--Bowdoin Street-Beacon Hill--Boston. Eighty bucks a week, can't beat that. Next door to me is a re-tired schoolteacher. She doesn't say much to me. She watches me pass through the crack of her opened door, then slams it when I am down the stairs. Real friendly joint.

I keep my life very ordered. Order for me is security. I am sure of some things. Like the fact I work five nights a week, and sleep during the day.

I don't have many friends to complicate things. I work a strange schedule anyway. I never gave much thought to working days.

Any women in my life? I thought you would get around to that. I haven't been with one in five years. They make me nervous. You know demands, expectations. Anyway...I work nights. You know how it is...

Tonight I am going to work as usual. The night shift is ideal for me. I work at a large psychiatric hospital just out-side the city: McFallow. At night there are no messy confrontations with patients. The frenzy of the day shift is a mere echo by now. The dust has settled, and for a good deal of the shift I am left alone. I read, bide my time. I occupy myself with thoughts of remote possibilities, or dead ends. Then before you know it morning comes.

Tonight is like any other night for me. I wake up slightly bloated, and it's dark out. The smell in my furnished room is stale. My flat is a study of disrepair with cracked ceilings, leaky faucets, a hot plate, not to mention a view of a back alley and brick wall.. Yet I feel comfortable here. It's my home. I sleep here, I eat here, and it is mine. This is where I go after work. Simple as that.

Soon I am walking down Charles Street. I climb up the stairs to catch the subway to Cambridge. I stand on the platform, and let the winter winds whip me across the face. I like the drama here. The expanse of the Charles River, the view of the stars unobstructed. It's almost like I am emerging from a tunnel of my own making. The air is fresh and bracing...my life has a horizon.

The train stops, and then hurdles across the choppy water, only to be sucked up in the bowels of Cambridge. I inhale the vaguely urinous air of the subway car. My window seat has a clear view of a passing pristine night sky. It seems like the stars are competing with the skyscrapers for attention...then all is a roar and black...

I check my bag. It contains: The New York Times, " A Portrait of a Lady," two magic markers, three yellow legal pads, two packs of Camels, a tube of hemorrhoid cream, and a Valium. Hey...whatever gets you though the night, right?

Years ago I went to work with nothing. Now-I find it necessary to carry things. I have to have them. I find myself anxious without them. I clutch my bag now, before it was loosely slung across my shoulder. I keep it. The shoulder strap won't break. It's so hard to let go of things. I guess working nights will do it to ya'.

The subway leaves me off in Harvard Square. I walk like a ghost through the crowds of young revelers, celebratory Harvard Students, and street hustlers who line the street. My eyes are fixed on the ground, rushing to catch the 73 bus to McFallow's.

McFallow's is on a hill in the town of Beltmore. Beltmore was once voted the most "boring" town in the state by the Boston Globe. But I guess that is a good place for a mental hospital to be located. There is a sort of hush here. The town could be described as "sedate", and McFallow was in the business of sedation.

Sybil greets me on the unit I worked, Trinap 3. She is the night nurse. She runs the shift. Like many of us she is a creature of the night. Her face is pale and drawn for lack of sunlight and sleep. Her body is bloated, its bulk sagging, hanging limply from her stooped frame. She seems at times to be in as much acute stress as her patient charges; alternating between agitation and distraction. She often demands my immediate attention, and dismisses me in the same breath. But she doesn't really bother me. Like the contents of my bag, she is a necessity. I like to know what to expect...no surprises, five nights a week, get my drift?

Sybil is sitting in her usual spot in the nursing station. She seems to be totally absorbed in her paper work. Her graying beehive hairstyle bouncing up and down, to and fro, behind the fortress of note books she is working on.

" How are you, Sybil?" I ask.

" Fine dear.. she replies, and then abruptly " You are not going to stand there all night are you!"

I have to laugh to myself. I find her perversity comical.

" Calm down the shift hasn't started yet," I respond.

" Of course... we must have lunch, one of these days. I know this cute little place in Newton Village..."

I usually shut her off by this time. She usually babbles on about her niece and her new husband, a "darling" antique store she found in Concord, or the incompetent people the nursing agency sends over.

She stops her late night stream of consciousness in mid sentence and says:

"You will be specialing a patient tonight."

Sybil then resumes her spiel, something about the lack of morality in young people today.

I am barely listening. Tonight I bless my good fortune. To '"special" a patient simply means to sit in a comfortable chair and watch an inert, sleeping or drugged body strapped to a foam mattress for a couple of hours. The patient is almost always asleep, and even if they are awake, they ramble on like Sybil. I just turn them off. I am free to read, work on my thesis, or reflect. I have been relieved from the normal tedious duties of the night shift. The symmetry between the patient and me is perfect. Both of us are in our little self-contained world. We are housed in a hushed and dim ward. I often check on these patients for breathing and vital signs. They are securely restrained by leather straps and their every need is met by the workers. They usually have been violent, but now they are sedated into a soothing haze. I almost envy them.

After pouring a cup of coffee that was consistently polluted by a terminally cheerful day nurse, I went down to check on the patient. He is a man about my age, with the sort of muscular torso that comes with hard labor rather than the measured repetition of a Nautilus machine. I check to see the restraints are secure. I am on edge with physically imposing clients. I have never been secure with my own physical capabilities. I am an oddly constructed man of narrow stooped shoulder, slightly bulging abdomen and spindly limbs. This guy could clearly eat me for lunch. Luckily he is asleep. I have some work I need to do.

I sit down in the chair, just outside the quiet room. I have to be able to see him breathing. Hours of spot-checking the rise and fall of his chest. Over the years I've seen all shapes and sizes. I've seen pigeon chests, barrel chests, concave chests, well-endowed women's chests rising and falling like slowly bouncing melons. What interests me about this person is his face. He is clearly Boston Irish. The standard package: hard blue eyes, thinning blond hair, the weathered skin of a laborer, or someone has a taste for the libations and smokes. I have a sense of unease about him. Even though he is asleep I have a sense of a feral, probing intelligence. I feel like the prey before he is eaten by the predator. I probably read too much. Working nights can do it to you.

About an hour into my shift I am totally absorbed in my work; cloistered on the ward, straining to find phallic imagery in the work of Henry James. This arcane study is the "meat" of my thesis. It is something that I have been working on fitfully for years. I feel like a weasel, squirreled away in some remote forest den, greedily digging out bits and pieces of sexual innuendo from the highly refined and mannered work of James.

" Writing your memoirs, chief?"

The voice comes as a cold shock. It is thickly accented, with a strong emphasis on the "r's" It comes barreling out of the room, derailing my chain of thought, insisting on my attention, intent on confrontation.

"Cat got your tongue, pal?"

"School work," I reply.

I wonder what he is doing up. I remember that Sybil said he can have no more medication. Maybe I can convince him to go to sleep. I don't want an all night dialogue.

" You really should get some rest. You need it," I say.

"Yeah, and what makes you a friggin' expert. You a head shrink or something?"

"No, I am a mental health generalist," I reply.

The patient snickers to himself. I fumble through my bag. The Valium is gone. I must have dropped it somewhere. I wish they would turn the heat down. It is so damn hot!

I see Steve come down the hall, checking each room compulsively. He walks down the ward deliberately. He stops at each room, holding the flashlight like a ray gun, shooting a beam of white light at each bed as if to keep aliens at bay. He is a diminutive man of about 30, has thick blond hair, and a baby face. He looks like an overgrown choirboy. He is sucking on some breath mints. A necessity, if you make a pit spot at the local watering hole before work. He smiles at me:

" Looks like you are here for the whole evening, old boy. We got a sick call. Sybil asked me to tell you," he says.

At another time I might have been happy with these prospects. But this guy I was specialing gives me the creeps. I'll ignore him. I'll shut him off. I'll make his words meaningless vibrations from his throat. I'll maintain my composure, an airtight vacuum. I will be in CONTROL of the situation. I can use a smoke. No hope for that. They have given me the chair...seven hours sitting here, with a gue- rilla. I'll bury my head in the notes. I'm trapped...

" That nurse on the second shift. Now I call that filly a fine piece of work. I went out with a chippie like that in Charlestown. She had a body on her that would give a stiff a hard on. What's her name?"

" Clovis. Listen it's really important that you get some sleep. I really can't talk about other staff," I answered.

" You got a girl, professor?"

"I don't think that's anything we should discuss.... try to sleep." I reply.

" Even money you don't. I figure you for a guy who runs the first time they pull down their pants."

He laughs nefariously. I squirm in my seat. The damn heat, can't they turn it the fuck down. My throat is beginning to tighten. I can't concentrate.

" That none of your concern, I'm sure. Please focus on yourself, that's what you are here for."

He laughs again. He seemed to enjoy this interrogation. I contin- ued to plead the fifth to no avail.

" How old are ya', bud?'

"Thirty Five. Are you satisfied. Please try to calm down. Please try to calm down."

" Working nights, living alone I bet. What do ya' do for kicks, stay inside and play with yourself," the patient sneers.

I reply: " My life is not your concern. I am going to stop this interaction."

" Stop This Interaction? You talk like you think your something. There ain't much difference between you and me. I'd say I probably should be in the chair watching you."

The time is two-thirty AM. It seems it will be five hours of torture. I am as much trapped as he. We are in the middle of a strange dance, and he is leading. I wish he could be quiet. Just shut up for a minute.

" Where do you live Mac?'

" A furnished room in town. Perhaps that fact will put you to sleep."

" Suicide suite, huh? Bet you have a few tumblers, shoot your wad, and say woe is me."

" My life is not your concern." I reply.

" Not that I give a shit. I just make it a hobby to figure out strange birds like you. Funny me down here and you up there. The only reason your ass ain't on the line is because of these four straps."

I will try to ignore him. I feel like a lab specimen, being dissected. I was trained to refocus the conversation to the patient. He is reducing my life to his pathetic vision. I work hard to keep things in their proper place. It is a precarious balance to maintain, yet I have achieved a fragile stasis. I now feel like a Blanche to this guy's Stanley.

" Me I am married, a few kids. I admit I hit the juice a little hard. We all have a few skeletons...know what I am saying. I don't regret much. I had a good time, bird dogging chicks, running with the boys playing the dogs at Wonderland."

" We are about the same age, ain't we Prof. A billard ball has more hair than you. Got a face that would make Igor look good. You are going nowhere fast Jack."

He seems to have a genius for picking out more sore spots. His perception is fine-tuned, and with laser accuracy he tears at me. It is a game to him, in which the stakes are higher for me. He has a need to get to me, a focus for his venom. I am his personal toilet bowl.

" More to life than those books you read friend. Working nights a long time?"

"Long enough." I say

" World goes by, and you sit in the dark. People make families, take vacations, maybe make some decent change. But you stay in the dark. A cheap room, a hot plate, some old picture of some girl who forgot your ugly mug a long time ago...What a waste..."

" Just shut up. Just shut up!" I was losing my composure.

He smiles widely. He got a rise from me. It as if he smells blood. This is his personal march to the sea. He has momentum on his side.

" Did I piss you off pal. Good. Now we are cookin' with Crisco. That's what you need. To get good and mad."

" He continues: " I know guys like you. Educated, working shit jobs. Think they are better because they read a few books. Sort of keeps them going. They wind up in some fleabag. The big decision in their lives is whether to order the meatloaf or pot- roast in the lo-cal diner."

I think to myself. What was it five years ago. There was a girl. She used to say I was special. I loved her. She made demands on me. I walked our apartment like a caged animal. There wasn't any defining incident in our break up. Just a slow fade out, and then a note: You're a special person, but its over, Don't call." I never saw her again. I even looked for her for a while. Not anymore, ancient history.

There was silence now. I looked up from my notes. He is smiling at me without warmth, without a trace of humor. It is a smile of a man who has the upper hand.

" So what is it Sherlock, you got something to hide?"

"I really must insist that you focus your energies on yourself. After all that's what you are here for."

My voice starts to quiver. This makes the patient perk up. He is almost coiled like a cat ready to spring.

" The question is why are you here? They had to drag me here kicking and screaming. I got a wife and kids to go to after I blow. You are staring at your navel every night. I think you found a rock to crawl under friend."

A decade. A decade of long nights. A long string of darkness. My eyes squinting in the early morning sunlight. The morning commuters and I are always in furious opposition, moving in different directions. The day in progress. I come home everyday and fall asleep to the din of talk radio. Disembodied voices that intertwine with my sleep. The night shift has always been my soft cushion to the frenzy of the world.

I found my eyes swelling with tears. There is a pit in my stomach as empty as my life. I am swaying back and forth in my chair. I hold my sorry body with my thin inadequate arms. I don't know how long I stayed this way...

The patient is asleep. He has a contented look on his face, like a baby fed and tucked in. He sleeps soundly. It is 7AM.

" You are relieved now." Steve said at the end of this long shift.

I walk down the bright hall. The morning light has generously filtered through the sterile ward. The day shift is in progress. I walk by them like a ghost.

" Leon, what are you doing?!" a day nurse asked.

The foam mattress supports my limp body well. My arms and legs are outstretched waiting for the leather straps. The sun shines through the screens illuminating the room giving it a divine glow.

" I've been relieved now. I've been relieved."

The End.

§

CHINATOWN

"Rockabye, they'll be a blanket to cover you, when you go down."
-- Robin Holcomb, Rockabye

By Lo Galluccio

Now, after 3 suicide attempts, I'm grounded by Chinatown: its fancy fans, frozen fish and money cats. Once I went looking for poison there. This time with friends – my grief disbanded – we talk about 18th century ladies who took arsenic to go pale.

Just a pinch or two, not enough to die.

There's Madame X on my gold-painted bathroom door in Manhattan. White as the moon, bending in a curve like S. S for snake. S for sophisticated. S for surreal.

In the Park I circled the big sycamore and heard music, Robin Holcomb from Iowa in my head. It led me back, back to your studio on 5th Street where I'd been a princess. There was a saint shining on the key ring you demanded back. I came to you naked under ivory raincoats and we made love. "It's spring," I pleaded. The music teasing my hair from the sycamore.

You still said, "No."

Twisting in strange sheets in St. Vincent's exile I suddenly knew what a prison can do to your soul. Yet when they dragged my friend Cecilia away screaming, she saw me mouth the words, "You'll be all right." from behind the TV room door.

In solitary, she woke up.

The dawn sparkled violet through the bathroom screen but I never wanted you to know. As sure as those hands played black and white keys like an angel all I wanted was:

to rockabye you and be free in Chinatown.

§

"Our Meeting:"

A Vision Of Van Gogh At Arles (2001)

Seeing him fight the darkness
by sticking lighted candles
on the round rim of his hat
so that the flashing strokes
of his brush can create this day's

third or fourth painting,
I--ablaze with joy--
shout across the shadows,
"You know everything
there is to know about me."

- Robert K. Johnson

"Last Night"

(October 18, 2001)

I saw a movie made
three or four years ago
that deftly used two hours

for a story that portrayed
life in a city school,
but a story pale in its powers

compared to the truth conveyed
in the film's split-second view
of what was once the Twin Towers.

- Robert K. Johnson

My Heart
for L.

If ever they trace the lines of my chest
with ink as you traced them with your tongue,
kiss me first. Hold my tongue to yours,
pull it until it goes numb. Paste your lips
to mine until I can taste your birth.
If ever they open me and the bluebirds
come rushing out, I want to hear you sing
in the flutter of wings. This is the way
things are healed. This is how the tired
travelers gaze into the eye to be sustained.

And when the blood goes rushing away
from me like children who have opened
a forbidden spout, touch something of mine.
Hold me that way to know that I want
to hold you more than life itself, but a choice
must be made. Some vinegar must go
where agony cries out already, enough.
I hang in the tiny crochet in feeble hands,
as they give me a stranger's heart.

If all of this is just a dream, and you fly
away from me before the gray takes over,
I will touch you everywhere I go.
I will declare the world your body and
christen our children in the air of names.

Afaa M. Weaver

INVITATION

nothing one can do
is ever going to be
enough, whether
as son, lover, drudge, parent, guardian
of the Word, the world
keeps coming around
for more, someone is always raiding
the fridge, or trying to
start something or dropping
hints or dead at one's feet, and time is not
on one's side--therefore take care
to love yourself
not least, let the world look after itself
now and then, buy an ice cream, settle back
with a cold beer, take in
a game, get into the swing
of that ass, the sweet breasts
of roses, after all, one is only
human, a puff
of elevated dust, in that shaft
of sunlight the ancestral
bones are dancing

- Doug Worth

Shopping

Pushing the cart from the main isle to the center
Almost striking the cart turning in,
I stop and look at her
Much as she looks at me
An awkward pause that seemed like forever
As I gazed into her eyes past age lines and sun damaged
skin
Revealing life had not been easy on her

I called her name as she called mine
Recognition of the eyes never seems to leave us
Histories exchanged we said our goodbyes
She as beautiful as that first day in Junior High
Handsome I once was, wondering if she thought so now.
The tastycakes in my cart suddenly were back on the shelf.

- G Emil Reutter

HIS DARLING

by Miriam Gallagher

She wasn't beautiful or elegant like the girls he'd admired, even worshipped, when he was twenty. But she was his Deirdre. He was always clear about the women in his life. Even in the early days whenever he fell for a girl it was final. Like his wife. Poor Mona. His darling till the day of her death and for a long time afterwards.

He'd always been protective towards Mona and wanted to bring her home from hospital so he could mind her himself. The doctor, however, told him firmly she'd be better off with proper medical care. Meaning he was incapable of minding his own wife and now would he please mind his own business and let the doctors get on with theirs. This only intensified his desire to protect her in her final struggle, driving him to placate the nurses with gifts, waylay the doctor for extra snippets of information and fiercely guard Mona from unwelcome visitors.

His sister was the worst offender. She'd arrive by stealth, creep into Mona's private room, jabber away about Reverend Mother's plans to renovate the convent or other such nonsense, and exhaust his wife, whose suffering was now on display for visitors. For a visitor was all his sister would ever be. They hadn't been a close family. Not such a bad thing. It meant that when he met and captured Mona he could devote his entire heart to her. She was breathtaking with her blue laughing eyes and bobbed hair. And what a voice! No wonder she was in constant demand at musical evenings. And what's more she could play the piano with finesse. As if tasting a vintage claret, he savoured the memory of those days when the house rang with music and laughter.

He poured a cup of tea. Plenty for one in the tiny teapot. After Mona died he'd sorted out the kitchen, using one place setting to save the good china. He stored her hoard of rice, lentils, tea, and tall brown bags of sugar in the top kitchen press, safe out of harm's way. What a divil for hoarding she was! 'You'll be glad of what's on the top shelf,' she often joked. Afterwards he hadn't the heart to interfere with her store of dried goods. However, when his sister swooped in 'to help' she discovered weevils in the rice and chastised him for harbouring germs. How dare she stand tiptoe on Mona's kitchen steps and peer into the Holy of Holies! He'd given her a right roasting for interference. Since that day she had never darkened his door, something for which he'd be eternally grateful.

After Mona's death people pitied him because he had to cook and clean for himself. They didn't know that menial tasks kept him sane when the ache in his heart became too great. He'd lived with the ache so long it now seemed part of him. At first when the wound was raw and smarting he'd clung to it as the one true feeling in his life. Then, when it dulled, he grew fearful that the only real part of her he possessed would disappear, leaving him to his solitary cups of tea and lonely evenings. He felt guilty when the wound became less sensitive to the touch. Gradually the nagging ache lessened. And then, one day, it was as if she had finally left.

He decided to sell the house and contacted an estate agent. He was expecting a crisp young man, eager for a quick sale but instead a pleasant looking girl arrived, neat and trim with her briefcase. They hit it off right away. She wanted to know why he was selling and went around the house touching things in a proprietary way that told him she knew quality when she came across it. He could see her approving glance giving the French clock the once over. He offered her a glass of the wine he'd brought back from Portugal. When they met again he might offer his own Chateau Lambay and chat about the wine club. Lord, how Mona loved her wine!

'The way I see it,' she asserted, 'most people sell because

they're forced to.' He nodded. How right she was! She laughed, 'I wouldn't want you selling for the wrong reasons.' He was surprised by her candour. 'But what about your commission?' he countered. 'Oh, I won't be with the firm much longer.' She sighed, 'I want to follow my dream.' He refilled their glasses. 'Yes?' During the pause that followed he waited in the absurd hope that she'd confide her dream to him, a perfect stranger. But that didn't come till later.

Over several visits Deirdre told him about herself. Her mother, who owned a small hotel down the country, needed her help during the busy season. As she craved independence, this was a cause of endless friction. So in order to avoid her mother's excessive demands she'd ended up in the city, taking the first job on offer but felt stifled by the commercial side of the property business. 'I'd love to open my own hotel and cook for people myself,' Deirdre confided. He nodded appreciatively, impressed by her enterprising spirit. 'I'd make people feel at home,' she added with shining eyes. ' I'm sure you would,' he offered and was touched by the warmth of her smile. Later she announced she was going to take evening classes in advanced cooking so that she'd be up to scratch for the challenge ahead.

He began having doubts about selling the house. Once someone expressed interest he raised the asking price. 'Take your time,' Deirdre advised him. Torn with the thought of moving to a strange place, he decided to take it off the market. 'I think you're doing the right thing,' she confirmed. 'Especially if your heart isn't in it.' So overnight the For Sale sign was removed.

He took his crockery to the sink and cleared away the bread, butter and honey, dusting the crumbs near the sugar bowl that hadn't moved from the same spot since he took over the house. Mona was forever fidgeting with the kitchen, disturbing its order so that one week they ate facing the garden, the next with their backs to it. And she couldn't keep a definite place for anything. He'd changed all that. Pleased, he noted the tidy sink, glinting draining board, marble topped table already set for his next meal, and felt the presence of order.

After he'd finished, from lifelong habit, he brushed his teeth. No fillings and every tooth in his head. Not like Mona. Lord, how she loved chocolates! Her eyes would light up whenever he'd bring her favourite box of Double Centres or bars of Toblerone.

At first she used visit him in his dreams every night, then less frequently. Often she was in green velvet and wore long silver earrings that dangled. She was as he had first known her-beautiful and beyond his reach--as she was now. When the dreams ceased he felt a new pang of guilt. The ache of her was gone, and then the dreams. He redoubled his efforts to lure her back, making a shrine of her picture in the sitting room, which he denuded of all other faces. In the evenings he would keep vigil, sitting in the burgundy velvet armchair she'd so desperately wanted, though the house bulged with enough chairs to seat a regiment.

Even after he'd taken the house off the market Deirdre continued to call. He was flattered and looked forward to her visits. She brought a slow, easy warmth into the house, dropping in unexpectedly on her way into town to the theatre or cinema. Sometimes she'd turn up for tea, bringing a cake or apple tart, promising to surprise him with haute cuisine once her advanced cookery course ended. Scoffing at homely dishes like bacon and cabbage, she produced a book with pictures of mouthwatering dishes that she would serve in her own hotel when the time was ripe. And, watching her gleaming eyes as she outlined her plans, he recognised her as a girl of spirit. If she wanted something she was sure to get it.

He murmured approvingly over images of boeuf en croute and cassoulet. When alone, however, he had to admit it was hard to beat a nice piece of collar of bacon. With the cabbage cooked in the bacon water. Wasn't he and the whole of Ireland reared on it? Indeed it was now his mainstay unless he took the bus into town for lunch at Bradley's staff canteen, where he was treated like royalty-though he'd never worked there. Simply turning up and smiling at the waitress had done the trick.

After her course ended, Deirdre, who needed to practise her culinary skills, offered to cook for him if he wished to entertain. He was delighted and flattered. Mona's idea of gastronomic efforts had been a tray of savouries at their musical evenings. In contrast his dear girl hadn't a note in her head but she was a dab hand at dinner parties, and soon his carefully selected guests were dazzled by her beef stroganoff and creme brulée. He was ashamed to find himself comparing these dishes with Mona's plain cooking for he considered loyalty one of the cardinal virtues. But the Mona he knew in the old days, the laughing singing Mona, would understand that he had to survive as best he could in a dead house full of empty fireplaces and the sound of soccer on the telly.

For too long he had brooded and now thanks to his dear girl he was literally reborn. People remarked on his zest for life. Neighbours, whose invitations tended to clash with Deirdre's visits were now finding their ministrations redundant.

As an attempt to repay her generosity he took her out to dinner. Well dressed and attentive to his needs, she was captivating company. He fancied other men envied him his young lively companion. Before long he was alternating suppers at home with meals in the latest restaurants, where he often arranged for her to inspect the kitchens. For she needed to keep abreast of culinary trends in order to follow her dream. Whenever he was invited anywhere he asked if he could bring his Deirdre and pined if he had to go alone.

He could barely wait for evening when she would call with a surprise. He wondered what delight she was planning for him now. For Christmas it had been a brandy glass, the perfect match of one given by a member of the family last year.

In the bedroom he selected a tie he'd bought recently. A bold red with yellow stripes. He would wear the new tie pin. A man could be dead long enough. 'Love me, dee-ee-ee-rest, love me,' he sang while he combed his hair. As he waited in the sitting room it struck him that a great part of the joy he derived from his dear girl lay in the sweet ache of anticipation. If she ever went away he'd miss that almost as much as her company. He turned on the telly - boon to the solitary. They'd bought it after Mona sold the piano. Lord, how she loved those weepy films! After watching a replay of highlights from a recent match he turned it off. The clock winked the remaining minutes at him. It was one of Mona's more successful buys. She was a terrible woman for bargains, always off to auctions down the country with one of her cronies. He'd shuddered when moth-eaten sofas, dressing tables and enormous wardrobes arrived by lorry, making their suburban home swell with furniture that belonged in a mansion. Yet, after she was gone he couldn't bring himself to remove her 'bargains.' And he had to admit she had an eye for smaller items – like the French clock that kept perfect time and was now ticking each minute until Deirdre's' visit. He put two glasses on the mahogany coffee table and brought cheese and wine from the kitchen. She might be peckish. He eyed his preparations approvingly. Maybe she'd stay longer this time. He smiled, anticipating an amiable chat over several glasses of wine, even half hoping for a minor crisis in her life. For these crises provided welcome opportunities to comfort her. Like the time her car was broken into and her handbag stolen. On the phone her voice had sounded full of unshed tears 'I don't know what to do. When I rang Daddy he ate the face off me.'

' Where are you?'

'At the flat.'

'Don't move. I'll be over in 10 minutes and you can tell me all about it then.'

Replacing the receiver, he'd secretly admitted it was asking for trouble to leave a handbag unattended in a car. Then, blessing his good fortune, he'd dashed from his telly to shield her from adversity.

Over coffee it all spilled out. 'You see I was out in Howth - with the chap at work I told you about. On the spur of the moment we decided to go for a walk. You know how these things happen.' He did indeed and listened intently as she continued, 'We went to the end of the pier and didn't notice the time passing.' Her eyes clouding over, she went on, 'When we got back the car window had been smashed and my bag taken. He brought me home by taxi and went off to tell the guards.'

'Don't worry your head, darling. I'll sort everything out for you.'

With a neighbour's help he'd managed to tow her car back to his own garage where he minded it jealously till it could be repaired.

Mention of the chap at work opened up the possibility of some young fellow laying claim to his Deirdre. He realized, of course, that such a lively girl would be surrounded by admirers. Indeed, the conquest of hugging so much of her time and talent to himself was heightened by the prospect of capturing her from rivals. Soon afterwards, he was forced to acknowledge the existence of such a rival when she brought him along one evening. Her shining eyes made him wonder how involved she was with this nondescript fellow, who'd made her throw caution to the winds and leave her handbag in the car, a silly thing for a sensible girl to do.

'Heard such a lot about you, sir. It's a great pleasure to meet you.' The fellow's tone was deferential, with the 'sir' trumpeting the gulf of years between them. Inwardly cursing the young man who could bring that gleam to her eyes, he'd made a special effort to be cheerful, exchanging pleasantries as they sipped drinks. Yet they'd barely arrived when it seemed they were off.

'What's your hurry?' he asked, trying to pour them another drink.

'Dan has an early start in the morning,' Deirdre explained.

So, in order that Dan might be fit for his early start, he'd gone for their coats. When he returned they were looking at Mona's picture.

'I was just saying that your wife must have been a very beautiful woman,' Dan offered.

'My wife was one in a million. A truly remarkable person.'

They'd stood for moment in silence, locked in their own thoughts.

Lately the young man hadn't been mentioned once in conversation and by this time could well be out of the picture. Out of sight, out of mind, he thought gratefully as things slipped deliciously back into how they'd been before.

The clock ticked away. It was only a question of time now. He glanced around. Everything shipshape. He sang:

'Just a song at twilight when the lights are low,

When the flickering shadows softly come and go.'

Though the heart is weary, sad the day and long,

Still to us at twilight comes –'

His heart fluttered as the bell rang. In the hall he hurriedly opened the door to his Deirdre. She had an unusual air of excitement about her.

'Come in, come in. Don't stand out here in the cold. Let me take your coat.' He led her into the sitting room and offered cheese and wine.

'I've eaten, thanks, but I'd love a glass of wine.'

They were seated on the sofa that belonged in a mansion when she showed him the ring. For a moment he felt as if someone had knocked the air out of his stomach and kept glancing from the cluster of diamonds to her face, unable to say anything.

'Isn't it gorgeous?' she breathed, admiring it with her eyes.

'Well, well, this is certainly a surprise,' he managed to say at last.

'I wanted you to be the first to know. Tell me, are you pleased? 'She was like a child telling a secret, eager and appealing, and looking into her eyes, he thought she'd never seemed so delectable and so beyond his reach.

'You know, my dear, there's no man at all who would be worthy of you.'

'Of course you'll be first to be asked to the wedding. Golly, what a lot of things to do.' As her eyes glazed over at the challenge ahead, he coughed, 'I suppose when you're married you'll soon forget all about your old friends.'

'Ah now,' she teased with a turn of the head that was at once perky and chiding. 'Sure I couldn't possibly forget you.'

Just as he was about to pour the wine she covered the glass with her hand. The diamonds winked at him, and in that moment he hated the hard little glittering pieces that would never leave her finger.

'I'd love another glass, honestly, but I really must go.'

In the hall he helped her into her coat. 'Call in soon again,' he commanded.

'I'm working down the country next week,' she replied.

'I'll miss you,' he sighed, 'You know I always love to see you.'

'Well, you'll have to wait till I get back,' she laughed before stepping through the hall door.

'Make it soon,' he urged, feeling a sudden rush of abandonment.

He waved her off down the garden path and in that gesture waved away his Deirdre as he had known her.

Alone in the silent house, he sang softly, 'When the flickering shadows softly come and go.' Back in the sitting room he stood, glass in hand, looking at the French clock and reflected that Mona's taste in clocks was exquisite.

§

Partner Swing

You in a tee-shirt— me in a flare skirt —
tap our toes to the beat of the bass
the prompter calls honor your partner
we're off in a fervor of pulse and whirl
join hands four to form a star
promenade down and come back home —
we pass over — they pass under—
clasp hands across for lady's chain
the flute notes fly —we weave a basket
the birdie hops in — the crow hops after
the piano keeps a steady beat
everyone dips — everyone dives
partners gypsy along the line —
a hint of jitterbug — a smatter of swing
a tat-tat-tat—a fling-fling-fling
we glisten and grin as the dance ends
with a partner swing.

- Molly Lynn Watt

Pub Dance

Dancing with you
is not hip-wrenching twists
as we gyrate to a flashing strobe
under a moon of mirrors.
Nor do we slow-grope to heaven
under crepe-paper streamers
in a chaperoned gym.
It's to the UM-pa-pa of the polka
played on the jukebox for a quarter —
your hands brace my hips
my arms encircle your neck —
we — the only dancers — grind up sawdust
on the floor of the Golden Eagle.

- Molly Lynn Watt

28th Century Milky Way Conference on Hieroglyph Philology. Paper 27-09:

By Edward Abrahamson

Decoding the Police Surveillance Tapes for Family Improvement; N. American Plastic-Magnetic Layer.

1.   **Abstract.** It is now clear from the decryption that the decline and fall of this once vigorous civilization resulted from pandemic attenuation of libido in 20th Century Baby Boomers.

To counter demographic consequences, the evidence shows authorities' valiant efforts to build community based holistic sex therapy establishments known as massage parlors and escort services.

In support of this more informed view, hear the following extract of the Police Surveillance Family Improvement Tapes:

2.   **May we help you?** Sure, lots of men
want to talk about family life. That's OK.
How many kids do you have?
Four? That's nice. Two boys. Wow. Full of mischief.
And two teenage cheerleaders. Cool.

 But you want the real doggie position?
Well sure, but.. how is it done at home?

Oh.. you get down on your knees and beg?

    And she rolls on her back and plays dead?

3. **A Glossary update..** with thanks to IGESS (Intra-Galactic Exchange for Scholarly Studies.) As translation from Latter Earth languages to Telepathic Texting is inexact, our graduate drones in penal service offer this short list; subject to debate and revision:

May We Help You?.. A cultivated invitation to open up.

Family Value.. A financial contract of marriage often following accidental procreation.

Family Life.. A series of noisy catastrophes followed by alcoholic stupor. Sometimes in reverse order.

Kids.. (Still under debate.) A sampling of those catastrophes.

Baby Boomers.. Those who suffered grievously from Family Life.

Sex Therapy.. Ancient cure and escape from Family Life.

Massage Parlor.. Tastefully decorated escape venue.

Escort Service.. (Nuances still under study by drones.) Believed to be another cure variation.

Doggie Position.. The Institute for Sex Therapy's oversubscribed graduate lab workshop.

Red Sky At Morning

By Charles F. Campbell

I had been 21 years old a whole month. Connie's surprise visit after boot camp had done many things, but mostly it made me realize that you cannot go back once the spell is broken. Even in the three months we had been apart, we had already changed so much, and our road was splitting faster with each passing day. We still wrote to each other, but neither of us said much romantic. We never mentioned a future that included us being together. The girl I had dated for months was now a pen pal at best. (Author's note: When I wrote this paragraph I believed what I said. I was totally wrong. I have corrected this in detail in the Connie at Christmas story. Part of the reason I am writing these is to explore my mind and my feelings, and this error is revealing so I shall leave it).

Three days after Christmas my ship was to set sail to the Far East for a nine month cruise. I had little idea what this entailed. I knew I was assigned to an ammunition ship and that we were going to be involved in the Vietnam War. Since boot camp, the ship had been in ship yards in San Francisco or undergoing training at sea preparing for the cruise. My life consisted of standing next to a steel wall all day smearing grey paint here and there. I had learned a basic truth about being in the military. It is mostly incredibly boring and routine stuff repeated over and over.

Imagining that I was about to face battle of some sort soon, I had managed to get leave to go home for five or six days at Christmas and see my parents one last time. I had three and a half more years to do in the Navy. I felt very alone and depressed. Yes, I was feeling wonderfully sorry for my-self. Knowing what I know now, I still feel sorry for myself back then. I wasn't a bad person. Hell, I had my Connie goodbye episode to prove that. I felt that my life was not my own any more, and maybe it wasn't.

So here I was, on leave in Victoria Texas. I was standing on the sidewalk outside the Student Union Building at a glorified High School called Victoria Junior College. I was facing something far more dangerous to a person like me than I have ever faced before or since, and she was beautiful. Her name was Ellen. We had been talking maybe ten minutes and I already knew two really important things. I knew that if I let myself, I would be tempting fate much more than I had ever allowed myself since the disastrous Suzy epi-sode. I also knew that it was only a matter of time until Ellen told me "Sorry Charlie. It is over". I prepared for that moment from the instant I met her. I was very wise for such a young and foolish fel-low.

Millions of little decisions had gotten me to this place and time. Mostly it was random chance and a nasty streak of meanness by fate that made me meet Ellen at this time, and in this place, and in such ultra-shitty circumstances. I am not sure why I was be-ing forced to make decisions I was not really ready to make and to think about choices that had no good answers.

Linda Whitty was the can opener fate decided to use to open this large can of beans. Whitty had lived next door to me for a few years my early teens or late adolescence. She was a few years younger than me, and I was not interested in girls yet, so we had no dealings that I can recall. I basically ignored her completely. Fast forward a few years, and son of a gun, it turns out she is a good friend of Connie's. I can only think of a couple of times I met Whitty when I was dating Connie, and that was on Connie's graduation night. Connie and I and Whitty and her boyfriend all went to the beach after the big graduation party. Another day shortly after that we all went to Mustang Beach for the day. This is pretty thin stuff for fate to use against me, but use it fate did.

I was sitting at the Corral drinking a Coke in my car. It was my first day home on leave. The Corral was a drive in restaurant that was the place to be in Victoria at that time. Sooner or later everybody under 25 or so drove through it to see who was out and about. Amazingly enough, Whitty just happened to drive through and see me. She parked beside me and excitedly asked if Connie was flying in to see me again. I told her no. I explained to Whitty that I was pretty much through with women until I was out of the Navy once and for all. The Navy was going to be a single lane road for this sailor for the duration. Yeah right. Apparently I can't pave for shit.

I was enjoying being talked to as Charlie Campbell instead of as some sailor, so I chattered on. I mentioned to Whitty that while I was not on the hunt for a new girlfriend, it would sure be nice to have a date or two just to have somebody to go to the movies with while I was home these few days. Unfortunately, Whitty had a really great idea. It seemed Whitty had a friend whose boyfriend was off at Fort Polk, or some such hell hole. Wouldn't it be keen if you two went out and had a few laughs until he got home? I thought this over as we talked, and for some impossible reason this made sense to me at the time. After all, the girl had a boyfriend so there was no chance of anything developing into a situation.

I had not seen the young lady yet, so I did not commit to anything at that time. Whitty understood and suggested I drop by the Student Union at 2 the next day to meet her and then decide what I wanted to do. We chatted a bit more and she left.

Now I must tell you something that I find impossible to believe even though I lived it and know that it is so. The next afternoon I was sitting at the Corral having a Coke, but the place was dead. It was almost 2. For some reason, I had forgotten that I was supposed to go meet this friend of Whitty's. Does this sound likely to you? It doesn't to me but I swear it is true. But even stranger, I suddenly started the car to go swing by the Student Union for no particular reason. I parked the car and strolled up the sidewalk to check out if anybody I knew was inside. The door opened as I neared it and out stepped a young woman and I instantly knew it had to be the girl Whitty had talked about. I recall feeling totally surprised that I had forgotten I was supposed to meet Whitty and a girl there.

"You must be Ellen," I said. Ok, so this was not Rick meeting Ilsa in Casablanca, but it was a start. I had thought I would be meeting both Whitty and Ellen when we set this up, but for some reason Whitty was no where in sight. I was on my own. If I had been 30 seconds later, Ellen would have reached her car and been gone, and I would have no story to write here. But fate had no intention of letting that happen.

How do I give you some small idea of what Ellen was like without drifting into sappy? I guess many people would find her unremarkable. She was cute enough, but not a stunner. She was slender with small breasts, but not a body to carve in stone. Her hair was long and a rich brown but millions of women had better. What attracted me to Ellen was that she had every single trait I found desirable in a woman, not the least of which was that she rapidly fell madly in love with me. Perhaps this happened often to Ellen. I do not know and I do not care. It took Connie flying to Victoria to see me after boot camp to convince me how much she cared for me. I had not a clue until then, because she kept me at such a distance. With Ellen, Her love was right there on her face with a smile that could make you forget to blink.

There was a song by Seals and Croft called "Get Closer" A line from it went, "Darling if you want me to be, closer to you, get closer to me". Within minutes of meeting her, Ellen probably could have described my pancreas in detail she was already so close to me. She was a wizard at getting closer to me.

Her most remarkable physical characteristic was her eyes. They were large and brown and soft. Her eyes were like a shining weather forecast. Ellen was not very subtle or mysterious. You could read what she was thinking and feeling all the time. There was a minor hit song by Nancy Sinatra called "Love Eyes". One of its lines was, "My world lies, right there in your love eyes". It was perfect for her. She was smart. She was popular (President of the Sophomore Class). She was extremely fun. She was passionate both romantically and in general. She had a fine sense of humor and was very playful.

This was heady stuff to a very alone sailor. Being closer to her was just about the best thing I could imagine at that time.

I am not so sure others saw her with such a happy eye as I did, because the down side was that she was extremely moody and could change from pure joy to what she called her "Holy Mother" mood in a nanosecond. I only saw glimpses of the "Holy Mother" mood because we were together such a short time. "Holy Mother" mood was going to be the end for us and there was not one thing I could do about it.

Fate had dropped this treasure chest of fun and sexy and love right into my shaky hands. Unfortunately, fate did it when I had three and a half more years left in the Navy. I was positive our relationship would not last 3 and one half months separated, much less three and a half years. The dynamism that made Ellen such a fun and thrilling person to know also was the seed of our own destruction. Realistically, there is no way someone that volatile could ever last over the long haul with me, even discounting the Navy time away. While she could fulfill so many of my deepest needs at that time, she would also take it all away between heartbeats.

Standing there on that sidewalk, I was taking this all in and trying to fathom what to do. You might ask why I did not take a pass on her, knowing as I did that this was a dead end street from moment one. Would you expect a diabetic to refuse insulin? You must remember, we would have a mere three dates at most and then her boyfriend would be home. What could happen in three measly days? I would then be off to Vietnam for nine months, and I was positive there was no way she would still be interested in me, especially after only 3 dates. I felt confident that I could manage to not go crazy for her in such a short time. It was a "can't lose" proposition. Sigh. Sure it was.

We could not stop talking to each other that day. It was like we knew it was a special moment where we were learning about each other and liking the other so damn much that we did not want it to end. In one of the ironies of the moment, she was wearing a sailor blouse that day. I pointed out that the kerchief was tied wrong and retied it for her. Whitty had not told her I was in the Navy so this is how she found that out. Finally, she really had to go and so I asked her to go out that night. Of course she said yes. I was already so confident and comfortable with her there was not the slightest doubt in my mind she might refuse.

We had three dates. They were standard Victoria dates of a movie and lots of driving around talking, followed by parking and making out. I wish I could tell you something special happened on them, or that she did something wonderful, but I have few distinct memories of them with two exceptions. One is that on the second and third dates I got to place my hand inside her blouse and bra upon a breast. This was way more than dandy. The second is that she had a strange way of kissing. She would open wide and then rotate her head around and around in a large orbit. It was like trying to kiss a merry-go-round horse. I finally managed to kind of trap her head in one place, close her jaws just a smidge with one hand, and stop the chase. Her kissing improved in a major way in a hurry. I never had a complaint about her kiss ability again.

Even though things went swell during our dates, I never pretended there were to be any more than the three. In fact, I seriously proposed that we enjoy the three and let that be it. She disagreed. She insisted that we write each other once I left, and at least have the possibility of a future time together. I readily agreed, but only with the clear understanding that we both knew that she would someday end it between us. She said that was ok, but that she hoped that day would never happen. Some of you may be thinking that I was creating a self fulfilling prophecy, and you might be right. All I know for sure is that it was my ticket to enjoy her company and not take a major hit at the inevitable end. Like most people, I was out to cover my own ass no matter what

Off to war I went. A few weeks later we arrived in Subic Bay Philippines and our mail caught up to us at last. At my first mail call in weeks, there were three letters from her. They were fantastic letters full of fun and enthusiasm and love and amazement. She loved me. She did not care about the cloudy future. She was enjoying loving me right then and there. I wrote her back of course and there we were. I still have every letter she ever sent me in a small packet in my bedside table to this day. For you snoopy types, I also have every letter Connie wrote me too, but not tied in a neat bundle in order like Ellen's.

I quickly discovered that fighting a war on an ammunition ship was not the stuff of legends. Basically, we loaded up with bombs and shells at the ammunition depot at Subic Bay for five days. We then went to the Gulf Of Tonkin for 35 days. In the Gulf there were always three aircraft carriers and lots of destroyers and cruisers using up bombs and ammunition at a hefty rate. Every day we would steam in a straight line at 12 knots and the combatants would steam alongside about 100 yards away. We would hook up winches to them and send across pallets of shells and bombs until they were replenished. My job was to stick steel straps through the pallets, and attach them to a hook on the winch lines for many hours a day. You repeated this sequence for nine or ten months, and then got to go back to the USA to get repaired and retrained for a few months so you could do it all again.

After a few weeks of this, I received an offer of a transfer from Deck Division, and all that wonderful pallet loading, to Operations Division to become a radarman. Apparently there was a better use for someone with an IQ above body temperature in the Navy after all. After some assorted infighting between officers, I was transferred. I began to learn how to be a radarman on the job, and through a correspondence course. In fact, the top picture of the Connie story shows me working on the book I was using to learn enough to pass the fleet exams, and get promoted to petty officer. But first … what a nasty phrase … I had to do my time on mess duty. You have heard of KP in the Army. Mess duty in the Navy was much the same. Each division on the ship supplied a man to work for three months helping feed the crew. We were basically there to clean up the mess decks and assist the professional cooks. My exciting life as a radarman quickly evolved into a deck mopping, coffee making, counter cleaning machine. It was actually a very simple job. I had to keep the salad area clean all day, and make coffee in these huge steel urn things. I had never made coffee in my life. In fact, I had never drunk a cup of coffee in my life, so you can imagine how it must have tasted. I simply poured in the grounds as I was shown and turned some valves. Nobody ever complained and they drank it like it was like the Nectar of the Gods. At least I never killed any of them.

The absolute worst thing about mess duty, besides the long hours, turned out to be a song. The mess deck had a jukebox like you used to see in cafes. It was a small unit listing 100 songs and you punched A12 to play a song over the mess deck sound system. It had been broken since I had been on the ship until some mega asshole IC man repaired it a week or two after I started mess duty. The song was, "Summer Wine" by Nancy Sinatra. Everybody loved it and everybody punched in its number (they had it memorized) when they passed by the unit. Apparently the system saved all the punched in requests. It was repeated over and over and over all day. All day. ALL DAY. I should have gotten a Purple Heart for enduring that.

One fine day we were in port at Subic Bay reloading for the next trip on line. I was wiping something to look busy when a man asked me if I was Campbell of Ops Division. I said I was, and he told me the Captain wanted to see me. Now this was more than a little puzzling for a deck swabbing nobody on mess duty. I went to Officer's Country and knocked on his door. He invited me in and immediately told me that the Red Cross had informed him that my father had suffered a massive heart attack and was not expected to live. He asked me if I wanted to go home on emergency leave and I mumbled yes. I had no idea I even could do such a thing.

Within an hour I had packed all my earthly possessions and walked off the ship onto the pier with no idea what to do next. Fortunately, another sailor was also going home for some reason. I hooked up with him since he knew how things worked. We got to Cubi Point Naval Air Station and snagged a small plane to Clark Air force Base where I was placed on top of the list for the next flight back to the USA. After sleeping in the terminal for almost a day, I was assigned a flight home. Oddly, I was also designated a United States Currier and issued a gun in a shoulder holster, and had diplomatic immunity for the trip. The trip up to Japan to re-fuel and then over the Arctic to a base near San Francisco is mostly a haze. I turned in the gun and stuff I was protecting, and after a brush with Customs, I was on my way again.

Talk about culture shock. I made it to the San Francisco air-port after a short stop for a shower at my aunt's house. Back then, people still dressed up to fly. I was surrounded by "round eyes", the very racist term we used for American women back then. They all looked spectacular. An extremely nice and adorable young girl of 16 or so sat beside me on the plane to Houston. She was so sweet and innocent and interested and nice to me. I cannot tell you how fondly I still think of her for her kind attention those few hours we were together. I wasn't running on empty. I was merely empty.

A friend of my father's met me in Houston and drove me to Victoria. I went directly to the hospital, and my dad was weak and pale and very glad to see me. Apparently his doctor had been enthusiastic with the negative diagnosis he had sent to my captain, and my father was actually responding well to treatment.

With that out of the way, the really important issue had to be faced. I was going to see Ellen again and it was not going to be for three skimpy days. Fate had dished up a major innovation to my Christmas three dates and get away plan. To say that I was conflicted about what would happen next is an understatement of the eternal sort. In a land of round eyes, I was going to face the roundest, brownest, loveliest eyes that I had never expected to see again.

When I called her and informed her I was in town, she was stunned to say the least. One of the first things she asked me was if I had gotten her letter. I had not. From her tone, I was positive it was the Dear John I had expected from the start. She told me to forget about it and we set up a date for that night. The letter did follow me to Victoria eventually, and indeed it was a so long sailor letter. Of course it was totally irrelevant by then.

We went out and the magic was still there. Houdini would have wept with envy.

I was scheduled for fifteen days leave. I drove to Beeville about one hundred miles from Victoria shortly after I arrived home because it had a Naval Air Station. I checked in there and got a fifteen day extension to my leave. I requested a hardship transfer to Beeville to serve out my time in the Navy. I failed to see why serving there instead of on an ammunition ship made any difference to them, since I would be fulfilling my military duties like the other sailors assigned there. The officer I talked to there thought I would make a fine radioman. I was not trying to shirk anything or get out of doing my duty. I just wanted to be closer to home and family and Ellen.

I headed back home with almost thirty days leave now, and some major problems about what to do about Ellen and me. While I still firmly believed that we could never last over the long haul, it looked like I would be getting a lot more enjoyment with her than I ever imagined. I had to convince myself that I could indulge myself with her, and still not go over the line and wind up devastated. I had had my one ration of out of control, stupid infatuation love already, and I was determined to never repeat it, or even come close. I honestly believed I could not survive another situation like that. Ellen was the ultimate test, the temptation, the road to hell. She was also adorable.

We had a month together. We did not have a date every night since she was still in college and needed to study, and besides, there was a good chance I would be stationed in Beeville. There was time, maybe lots of time. We did spend a great deal of time together because we enjoyed being together so much. There is little I can tell you about our dates because they were so unremarkable. What we did was not the issue. Being with her was the joy. It was all very relaxed and so much fun. We actually got to know one another and liked each other more every day. This is when the "Love Eyes" song was playing on the radio, and I would sing it badly each time it was played, but with enthusiasm.

Most of what we did is now a blur, but two moments stand out clearly and boldly in my memory. I have no idea why they are so significant out of all the other moments we shared. I offer them to you in hopes they might give you some insights that I cannot explain.

We went to the Lone Tree Drive-in Theater. The movie we would not be watching was called "Mondo Carne" which I think translates into World Meat. It was some long forgotten shock flick that turned out to be a gruesome, messy, bloody pile of icky in the brief scenes I did watch. A huge Texas size thunderstorm blew in shortly after it started and it poured like Niagara Falls for ages. Most people left and went home. Fire and thunder raced across the sky as the rain beat on the car like a million tiny jackhammers. My car had a long, wide bench front seat that I had pushed all the way back. There was plenty of room between me and the steering wheel. Ellen lay across my lap with her head on the driver's side door. She was naked from the waist up. We kissed and I stroked her while the storm raged against the windows. There was none of the drama and indecision like on my last night with Connie. I had no intention of having sex with Ellen. I wanted it to be positively impossible for me to father a child with her. This had nothing to do with morality. This was my way of assuring that I had a chance for future happiness after she would dump me. It was the most relaxed and open I could possibly feel with a woman in that situation given my internal complexities. Her trust and complete faith in me at that moment was also quite touching. My hands told me she was not tense and afraid one whit. It may be the one moment in my life I let myself feel true happiness that others seem able to enjoy at will. No matter what else Ellen might say or do to me the rest of my life, that moment earned her a pass in my book.

The other moment worth remembering is much quieter and less dramatic. It was a warm afternoon. We were either in my parent's back yard or her back yard, sitting on a garden bench or porch swing. I lay down on the hard bench on my back, and placed my head in her lap as she sat there. I closed my eyes and let my head feel her warm, soft body and legs. She took her hand and slowly stroked my head. It felt grand. Vietnam, the Navy, my father's heart attack, hardship transfers, they all faded to vapor. We were alone sharing this moment, and I was able to stop thinking for once and merely enjoy the cool touch of her hand in my hair. Her loving hand healed some of the hurt of my own making I carried deep inside myself. I have never been more at peace with myself and the world than at that brief moment. I had gotten closer to her, closer than anybody in my life and it was wonderful. I cannot tell you how much it meant to me. I simply have no words good enough.

I had my month of joy. My father recovered and came home. It turned out he lived 32 more healthy and happy years, and never had heart trouble again. I do have to tell you the one rather unkind thing Connie did to me that month. She called me out of the blue and announced she was at the Victoria Airport, and that I should come pick her up. I sputtered a bit and then she told me she was kidding. Apparently Whitty had told her about Ellen and me. I told her that, yes indeed, I was dating Ellen and I assumed she was dating boys up there too. We had a small debate, and thus ended our writing to each other for a while. It was the only mean thing I ever saw Connie do. I was sorry I saw it.

As you know from the Connie story, I eventually returned to Beeville and discovered that my request for a transfer was denied. I suppose I should have been more upset and requested an appeal or something. I received no explanation why it was denied. I was told to return to my ship. Looking back, I am sure that I was somewhat relieved it was denied. It solved my long term problem of what to do about Ellen. Additionally, I had had this perfect month that I knew was not sustainable. So far I had managed to not slip and let Ellen overwhelm me and start making major mistakes. I was sure I was running out of strength though. "Holy Mother" had also appeared in brief snatches the last few days we had together. Perhaps I even justified it by asserting that it was best for Ellen to drop me and move on with her life. At any rate, I sort of went home and told them all the bad news. I have no memory of my last night with Ellen. I had three years left in the Navy.

I returned to San Francisco and was put on another ammunition ship called the Pyro that was about to go to the Far East. I was immediately assigned to more mess duty. I was given the scullery job and washed food trays all the way across the Pacific Ocean. Eventually I returned to the Mauna Kea and they were shocked to see me. Nobody believed I would ever return to the ship. They kindly decided I had done my share of mess duty finally, and I started becoming a Radarman.

Her letters were sweet and tender and sad as she struggled to deal with the separation and loss. She became buddies with my father and would drop by and visit him now and then. They would take walks to strengthen his heart. My mother would sometimes call her to see if she had heard from me lately when I failed to write for a while. It was all rather surreal. I could only helplessly read her sinking into deeper depression and sadness, and I tried to write her things to help her make this transition. I guess the prospect of the transfer had allowed her to commit even more than before, and now she was suffering for loving me. I felt terrible about it.

Eventually, they let us go back to the USA. I had gone in the hole on leave days so could not go to Victoria immediately when we returned. Ellen and I wrote, and I called her now and then, but long distance was very expensive thanks to Ma Bell's monopoly at the time. Another Christmas approached and I finally had a few days leave on the books, and they gave me a few extra, so I was readying to see Ellen once again.

A week before I was to go home, I got a letter. It was vague and a different tone from the previous ones she had sent me. I went to a pay phone on the dock and called her to ask what was wrong. She was evasive, and troubled, and made little sense. She said we could talk about it when I got home, and that maybe it was nothing. I knew right then that this was a bullet I was not going to be able to dodge like I had last spring. It was a very slow week of waiting.

The familiar, potholed streets of Victoria once again rolled under my tires on the way to pick up Ellen my first night home. I had called her to finalize the plans for our date, but I do not recall anything that was said. She looked as lovely as ever, but the spark was not there when I finally saw her. She was not cold so much as distracted and quiet as we met in her living room. We got in my car and headed down town for the Uptown Theater to see some movie or other. The night was very cold for south Texas, and under the circumstances I felt a drive-in movie was not a great option. As I drove along I made several attempts to make small talk. She just sat there looking very uncomfortable and made little effort to respond. I finally became frustrated as we drove down Main Street, and I pulled the car onto a side road and parked next to an old appliance store.

I turned to her and gave her my full attention. "Ok, what is wrong," I asked knowing the answer.

I don't recall how she put it. I have a vague recollection of her describing how painful it was to be alone and miss me, and how she had to concentrate on her studies and so forth. It does not really matter what the reason was. She truly looked sad and miserable, and I give her full credit for doing it to my face, and not in a letter or on the phone. I do not think she enjoyed doing this one iota. I had been preparing for this moment for months, so I pretty much said all the things I had been practicing in my mind. I assured her I understood and felt no malice at all. In fact, I had predicted this moment from our first date. She replied that she knew I had predicted this and that made it all that more difficult for her. I told her that I understood completely. I was not angry at her. Of course I was disappointed to lose her and her wonderful companionship, and her soft lips and body, and all the smiles and fun that would never happen in my life now. I was not the right man for her really, and she was not the right woman for me really. The differences that meant so little now would have grown very important down the road. I am sure I said stuff like this to her. I even believed it I guess. Regardless, we got through it without tears and recriminations.

I suggested we go ahead and go to the movie. Yes, I admit this is rather pathetic. I had just been tenderly dropped, and was clinging on to have a few more minutes with her. While I was not going to become suicidal over this development, it was still going to be a mighty lonely few years ahead. Connie was gone and Ellen was my last weak grasp on something in my life not Navy and Vietnam related. I was about to become just another guy in a white sailor suit to everybody in the world except my family.

She paused a moment and then said. "No. You better take me home."

I said, "Ok" and started the car.

I noted that she had not moved away from me during all this, and was still sitting in the middle of the seat right next to me. I would like to think this was a positive sign. On good days I sometimes would think that maybe she wanted to go home right away for fear that, the longer she was with me, the more the temptation to slip back. Then we would have had yet another year of misery apart. It is a nice theory, but I did not have many good days anyway.

I drove like a ninety year old widow in her new Cadillac. Every red light was a victory. Every green light I made was a defeat. The silence in the car was so intense I had to crack a window to let some of it out. The contrast to our normal selves was more than obvious. One can prepare for an event a lifetime and still be overwhelmed. I contemplated perhaps making a bigger effort to keep her but decided that it was probably stupid and unfair. She had looked me in the eye and showed a lot of respect that night. The right side of my body still touched her. She deserved to have her way.

I had spent so much time driving so slowly and absorbing these last minutes with her that I had not planned what to do once we reached her house. Try as I might, we finally arrived. We got out of the car and I walked her to her door. I am sure I said something corny like if you ever need me etc. She looked so small and sad in her coat.

Well, this was it. I just wanted to hold her one last time but that seemed impossible now. I raised my hand and gently placed it on the back of her head. I slowly leaned forward and softly kissed her forehead. I lingered several seconds making it count. That last touch had to last a lifetime.

I leaned back and said, "Goodbye Ellen."

I think she replied, "Goodbye Charlie"

I turned and walked back to my car. With Connie I had leaned against the car and smoked a cigarette. Not wishing to repeat myself, I sat on the trunk of the car and smoked a cigarette. Obviously, practice does not make perfect when it comes to goodbyes. They lived just outside of town on the Hallettsville highway. An occasional car would go zooming past, and I speculated if they saw me sitting there in the cold night air smoking my cigarette. I finished it but felt reluctant to move yet. I wish I could remember what I was thinking. I pulled my coat a bit tighter around me and looked at the sky. It was a clear night but there seemed to be so few stars in this sky. One of the best things about the Navy was the night sky. Navy ships run darkened except for required navigation lights, and these red globed lights in most work spaces. In the middle of the ocean the air is perfectly clear and pollution free. As a result, the stars are spectacular. They are clear and bright and look close enough to touch. There were millions more of them in the sky than I had ever seen before. For the first time I could clearly see the intense band of the Milky Way stretch from horizon to horizon. You could almost read your heart by the starlight out there.

The Victoria sky looked so very weak and drab. I decided to do something dramatic, so I gave the sky the finger. This felt rather stupid so I stopped. So much for drama.

I think I had another cigarette, feeling Ellen deserved two to Connie's one. I guess I suck at symbolism too.

Eventually, I had to go. I drove to the Corral and had a Coke and watched couples drive through. I spent the rest of the night driving around all the streets I would have driven Ellen around after the movie. I drove around a lot that Christmas. There was not much else to do. I still had two and a half years left in the navy.

I returned to my ship and we returned to Vietnam. That spring I managed to pass the fleet wide exams and became a Radarman third class petty officer. We were supposed to wait a year before being allowed to take the second class test, but a spat broke out between two lifers running the radar gang and the electronics technician gang, and I wound up taking the test only six months later thanks to ship politics. We were steaming into San Francisco Bay following our second full cruise and they brought the mail aboard early on the pilot boat. The results of the tests had come in and they read them over the ships loud speakers. To my amazement, I had passed. I had gone from bottom of the barrel to almost the top in six months. I had learned it all from a book, and I knew how under trained I actually was. It is fortunate that nothing major ever happened requiring a real radarman the rest of my time in the service.

The only other significant event that year was that I had written Connie's father a letter sort of apologizing if I had hurt his daughter in any way. Obviously it was a lame attempt to try and contact Connie in some manner, and to her eternal credit, she wrote to me. Once again I had my pen pal. I feel I always badly underestimated Connie. She was a very good person.

After my promotions and completion of the second cruise, there was another Christmas and another leave in Victoria. After a few days home, I called Ellen one night. I asked her if she still had an 8x10 picture I had given her of me. She said she had it, so I asked if I could have it back. She asked why, and I told her that she probably had no use for it any more, and my mom would love to have it. She said ok and I drove to her house. Obviously this was a lame excuse to see her one last time. We met. We were cordial. She gave me my picture. I gave her the picture she had given me of her that I had pasted above my bunk and looked at daily for all those months. I tried to act charming and friendly and I think I pulled it off. I left.

A few days after Christmas, I caught a plane to West Virginia to visit Connie. Once we were corresponding again, I had asked if I could come see her. She had agreed. Those few days with Connie were so very important to me getting through the rest of my time in the Navy. Thank you Connie. Thank you. You were more than I ever deserved.

Within two weeks, I saw the two women who had dominated my life for years for the last time. I still had a year and a half left in the Navy.

Now in a normal life, in a normal time, that should be the end to the story. The discerning reader has already noticed that there are more paragraphs below. Fate insisted this not be a simple ending. I have no idea why this rather sweet story had to have such a strange ending, but so be it.

Another year and another cruise came and went. Nothing remarkable happened. The picture at the bottom of the Connie story was taken in Hong Kong in the middle of this cruise. Perhaps you can understand why I look so changed from the top one now.

I wrote Connie fitfully. Near the end of the cruise, we received the most wonderful news I could ever imagine. The Navy was reducing its forces and I was to be let out 3 months early. Ninety days may not seem like much, but it was like finding a cream that instantly healed terrible sunburn. I would get out in March instead of June, and thus miss having to start the next cruise. By this time I was the senior Radarman on the ship and would have had to run everything. This was not a good idea for me or the Navy I assure you.

I did fly home for Christmas and surprised my parents anyway. I drove around most of the time. I had three months left in the Navy.

The day of my discharge mercifully arrived. I had already packed my stuff off the ship in my car the night before. I picked up my papers at the ship's office, walked to the quarterdeck, and was signed off the ship and out of the active Navy. My green ID card became red. It was a bright and sunny day. The ship was at a pier in the repair yards in Vallejo California. It was an odd feeling to be leaving the ship that had been my home for so long. I had lived for this day relentlessly for four years, but I was feeling strangely empty. I walked down the accommodation ladder and down the pier. Just as I did with Connie and Ellen, I did not look back. With a stroke of innovation, I did not smoke a cigarette when I reached my car. I had zero days left in the Navy ... at last.

After a few weeks of halfhearted job hunting in the Bay area, I drove home to Victoria. I got a job driving a fertilizer truck to fill in the time before I went back to college. I was back at the Corral and watching the world drive by nightly. My mother had told me that Ellen's wedding announcement was in the local newspaper. She was marrying some guy she met in college at Kerrville. I had arrived back in town a couple of months before the nuptials.

One day a friend of Ellen's I knew slightly from the magic month stopped by the Corral and began talking with me. I forget her name, but will call her Miss X for convenience. She was a nice enough girl, and we talked often when we ran into each other. One night we even went back to my folk's place, and played strip poker and made out a little bit. Even in Victoria, four years had made some changes in the social rules.

She talked a lot about Ellen and the wedding coming up, and I enjoyed the insights on Ellen's life. There was a guy who hung out at the Corral almost as much as I did named Robert Pollard. He also knew Miss X, and through her we began to talk and become buddies. He was a nice enough fellow and we got along well.

One night Miss X said she had something she wanted to ask me. I said ok. She told me that Ellen asserted that I had freaked out on the night we broke up. She claimed Ellen said that I had a gun and had threatened to shoot either her or myself. I forget which. She also said that now that she knew me better, this seemed highly unlikely. I was totally amazed of course. I told her the story I have told you here, and she thought that made a lot more sense. Miss X also reported that Ellen was very worried that I might do something to wreck her wedding. This was more incredible news to me. I could not imagine destroying a special moment in a girl's life like that. I assured Miss X that I would not do such a thing, and please tell Ellen not to worry.

This news really freaked me out a little. I could not imagine why Ellen would make up such a story about me. Maybe Miss X was a liar, but why? Maybe Ellen had flipped out for some reason. Maybe I had angered her by not fighting to keep her more or something. I simply had no idea what to make of it. I did not care if a few people thought I was a crazy man, but this would make my time with Ellen a bit tainted.

Then fate dropped the other shoe. One night Pollard and I were sitting in my car at the Corral talking. I forget what was said exactly, but suddenly I realized that he had dated Ellen. I stayed casual and tried to find out when he had dated her and, you guessed it, he was the man Ellen left me for. My mind was somehow able to digest this amazing fact and remain functioning. If I was writing fiction, my editor would be drawing a line through all this as impossibly improbable. It was obvious he had no idea who I was. Apparently Ellen had only told him she broke up with some sailor but had not mentioned my name. I finally told him who I was and he was as amazed as I was. It turned out that Mister Pollard was not nearly so kindly disposed about Ellen. Sadly, he must have reached for the dream and taken it hard when it all crumbled. I found myself in the awkward position of wanting to hear more about them, but also having a great unease about actually finding out anything too personal. Of course I was very curious if she had said anything about me to him. I think he may have said a few things but I do not have a clear memory of him doing so, thus I shall not speculate. Those memories might be wishful thinking.

We stayed buddies and talked about her sporadically. He dropped a few hints about doing something at her wedding in a kidding way, and I did not bite. I understood his bitterness completely. I knew how big a loss it was to lose Ellen only too well. We were in a very exclusive club, and the dues were extremely high. The whole story about Ellen thinking I might disrupt her wedding now made a lot more sense. Her friend must have told her that Pollard and I were friends. She knew us both very well, and understandably might be suspicious we might be plotting something.

When I told Miss X that I had found out about Pollard and Ellen, she laughed. She said they all wondered how long it would take before we found out.

This did not give me a great deal of confidence in Miss X and her other story about my last night with Ellen. I decided that I wanted to ask Ellen about all this, and clear the air once and for all. I drove to a very special telephone booth that played a critical role in my life before Ellen, even before Connie, and called her number.

Her sister answered and I asked to talk to Ellen. When Ellen came on, I told her the story Miss X had told me, and asked her if it was true. Ellen flatly denied that she had done such a thing. I told her that I didn't believe that she would, but wanted to hear it directly from her. She said she had no idea why Miss X would tell such a story. I also assured Ellen I would not be harming her wedding in any way. She said that she knew I would not do such a thing. That was the last time I ever heard her voice.

A week later I called Connie and asked if I could drive up and see her. Connie gave me excuses. We had a small fight. That was the last time I ever heard her voice.

These are my memories from forty years ago. While I believe them to be completely accurate, that does not mean events and details happened exactly as I described them here. The other participants in the story may have slightly or even dramatically different versions. All I can say is that I made no effort to make anybody, including myself, look better or worse.

When I started this story, I thought it was going to be about my time with Ellen. As I wrote it, Connie kept becoming a major player in the narrative. Now that it is complete, I see that it has become more about my struggle to get through the four years of the Navy, and the crucial role these two women played in helping me accomplish this. I doubt I could have managed it without them.

You have probably noticed that I have not mentioned the world events swirling around me during this time. They are off stage players in my story. The war, the protests and the politics all played a role, but I leave it to you to form your own opinions about those issues. The reality of my life then was that my life was my ship. We were completely cut off from the world most of the time because communications were very limited in those days. I found that even when we were back in the States, I stopped following the news. It never reflected what I had seen with my own eyes, so it seemed pointless. My world depended upon my ship and my shipmates, and my tenuous links to Connie and Ellen.

You are reading this story through the voice of an older man. I cannot recreate the man I was, and the way I felt accurately now, because I know how the story ended, and what a happy life I have lived. Nothing felt so calm and certain back then. I was, and am, a passionate man who fears his passion so much he has devoted his life to controlling it. It is what I feel I had to do.

I do not know if it was dumb luck or some odd quirk of my personality that has allowed me to stumble across such amazing women in my lifetime. While there have not been many women in my life, the quality has been extraordinary. My wife and I have been married more than thirty years now, and much of the credit goes to what I learned from Connie and Ellen. The fact these wonderful people loved me and cared for me so much astounds me. It does not matter that the Connie and Ellen parts of my life ended on a slightly down note. Those details do not matter now at all. They gave me so very much, when I needed so very much. I hope I gave them something in return.

§

Charles F. Campbell as a young man

Come either way

Take the red line to the end—
step out and cross
the field, but oh! before you do,
see herons fly above, and hear
the red-winged blackbird's watery call,
and wait—a rabbit or a snake might cross;
then see the old man dance
his meditation in the sun,
and look—Sumac! Yarrow! Queen Anne's Lace!
let earth-ground work into your soles, then circle
past the honeysuckle-laced fence
(save this scent for me), the greenhouse
where weeds announce abandonment
and passion flowers mate with Heavenly Blues;
inhale the tended plots of squash
and marigold, and pluck
the words that prance across your heart
and say your poem (sing it!)
and here, almost at the end,
you'll find my house:
the blue one with red roses and a picket fence.

Or.

If you take the Harley—come through Harvard Square,
wind past Benny's for a smoothie (double mango, extra
sugar), stay to hear the drummer, get on Mass Ave, go past
Harvard Law, DEAF CHILD sign, pick up a video (surprise
me), pop into Wolf's Mystery Books (see if there's any james
cain) and at Tuscan Farms, stop! (eggplant for the grill); go
past Jack's Gas (you have to check the tires on my car); at
Norton's Liquors—keep going—until you hit Collaborative
Psychotherapy (boost self-esteem, they promise); you'll see
Mrs. Welch's two-family (remember I told you about her,
she's ninety, was born and raised nine kids here?); keep past
the fuscia storefront, the fortune-teller (be careful with your
heart, she says), and the next liquor store (keep going), and
City Hardware (don't forget the washer for my sink), Fast
Phil's Cuts (wash my hair tonight and I'll shave you in the
morning), turn at the dirt lot by the old gas station (call me
from the pay phone if it's working), past Aristocratic Auto,
Rent-Me Family-Limo, the condemned house, and the second one in is my house (pull into the driveway and look
up—Nice Guy Eddie's watching for you from my bedroom):
the blue one with red roses and a picket fence.

Come either way.

- Varsha Kukafka

Hunter Moon (Chapter 3)

from a novel by Anne Brudevold

Rain poured for the next week. Ray liked the repetitive sound on his roof as he worked at the anvil and forge. His thoughts turned to the Nunotuck River, where he and his buddy Bacon were planning a canoe trip that weekend. Gentle as the rain sounded on his roof now, it was reving the river up, for sure. Ray was starting a new order. A Texan wanted a utility knife for himself and one for his wife.

Ray did not like to repeat designs. He had done hundreds of utility knives in the past. This blade would be longer and thicker, the point narrower and sharper, the handgrips more defined. Ray usually filled an order then made it into a series, with enough differences so the customer still got a unique knife. The Texan had huge hands, and his wife had tiny hands. Ray drew the two designs to size, and then drew a series of generic utility knives based on the design, considered the balance, the weight, the metal, and handles. He checked his supply room for oil, steel bars, walnut burl, and deer horn. He called Miranda to ask her if she was free to engrave a series of utility knives in a few weeks. The Texan did not want engravings. However, many tourists liked a design on the blade. She drew things like Victorian women in a flowing dresses, nature designs, or Native American symbols.

"Sure," Miranda said. They had discussed going into business together, but nothing had come of it yet. It wasn't often that Ray wanted his knives engraved.

The phone rang. "Still up for the trip tomorrow? Bacon asked.

Ray had known Bacon since childhood. They had played together as kids, and, as teenagers, had tracked deer, moose and bear.

Bacon was totally at home in the wild. Ray hadn't been surprised when Bacon became officially registered as a Maine guide. Bacon had a gift for organizing and leading. He had been known to get lost, and he claimed he did it on purpose, for the pleasure of finding his way again. Ray believed that. Bacon liked finding solutions to problems, and he was good at it. Ray trusted Bacon as a friend, canoeing companion, and wilderness guide more than he trusted anyone else. It was not in Ray's character to trust anyone completely.

Truth be told, Ray had been thinking about cancelling this trip, because of the rains. The river would be swollen and the canoeing might get ugly. It was crazy that with this weather, Bacon wanted to do the most dangerous section of river, the Falls, which they had never done. Ray remembered Sage's prophecy. "I see death." He thought about it. He saw himself in his workshop for the next few weeks, grinding out knives in a routine that while fascinating to him, also brought out his dark side –the lust to do something different, something dangerous. The adventure-seeking, death defying Ray.

"Sure, we're on." Ray answered. He didn't even want to think about his doubts. "Meet you at the boat landing 8 a.m." The telephone connection crackled, and then cut off.

It was ten o'clock, time to turn in. Ray made sure everything in his workshop was exactly in place. He went into his living room, opened the closet door, and took out his knapsack and

canoe gear. He and Bacon went out on the river so often, he had things he needed for this trip ready in a few minutes. He climbed into bed and sank slowly into sleep, satisfied that he had put in a full day's work. He would start cutting the steel for the new order of knives next week. He had worked a full week. Tomorrow would be play.

In a light sleep, still hovering between reality and the unconscious, He dreamed. Three loons swam on a lake. They whooped a few times, and then began the unearthly chuckle that had given the birds their name and led to the expression "loony." In the dream, Ray didn't think the loons were crazy. He thought they were laughing at humans and their futile endeavors. One loon dived

under water and stayed for a long time. One loon had a baby on its back. She tipped it over, and it paddled a few strokes before scrambling up to its mother's back again. The third loon swam to an island, and disappeared. .

Ray woke at 6 a.m. He loaded his gear in the truck, hit the road and made for the river. He parked his truck at the boat landing. Bacon had already arrived and was stowing gear under the seats of the canoe. It reassured Ray. A good guide should always be ahead of you. Even in the informal, friendly trips Ray and Bacon took together, Bacon was ever the professional.

Water lapped over the launching dock and overflowed the banks. The currents sputtered and frothed. The marking post was completely covered -- the previous high water mark was under water. Bacon etched another, near the top of the post. It was raining again today. Ray buttoned the collar of his shirt and zipped his hunter- orange waterproof windbreaker up to his chin. He remembered last spring, when he had nearly died on one of Bacon's rafting tours. That had been on another stretch of the river. It had not been Bacon's fault. The woman sitting next to Ray had lost her balance, slid across the raft and pushed Ray overboard into thirty-five degree water so turbulent they hadn't even seen him go under. He tossed about for what seemed a lifetime before being grabbed and hauled to safety. He had had such a headache he thought his head would explode.

Ray tightened the drawstrings on his jacket hood and said to

Bacon, "I don't know about chancing the Falls today. The water's high."

Bacon continued loading. "I told you before. We have exact directions from someone who did it. If it looks too dangerous, we can always portage around the Falls. You remember the directions?

"Yeah," Ray said. "Strong right before the falls at your signal."

"What food did you bring?" Bacon slid Ray's duffel bag under the prow seat.

"Fitness bars," Ray answered.

"That cardboard shit? I should have known." Bacon fancied himself a gourmet. Ray wouldn't be surprised if he had managed to slip a bottle of Chablis or a toothpick hors d'oeuvre on board. It made him a popular guide with wealthy tenderfoot yuppies. Both Bacon and his wife loved to cook and they loved to eat. Bacon stowed a small package in a corner of the bow. "This is Rose's chicken cacciatore. She dehydrated it so it fits into a sandwich bag! We can rehydrate it and in twenty minutes we'll be eating at a four star restaurant."

"I can't wait," Ray said. His tastes ran more to plain, especially since his divorce. He did love good food, but it was no fun to cook for yourself. Better to pare things down. Cans. Jars. Fast food restaurants.

They floated the canoe and climbed in. It bucked evenly up and down. Ray made up in mass what Bacon took in height. They had no problem switching bow and stern. They were complete opposites, and that was probably why they got along so well. Bacon's hair, thick and Indian black blew straight up in the wind. Ray's windbreaker hood covered a bald spot, ringed by a short, neat wreath going gray. His hair used to be brown and he had worn it long like a hippy.

Bacon was tall, rangy and dusky, Ray was olive-skinned, almost Mediterranean looking, and short, with a massive muscled chest, developed from blacksmithing.

Bacon took stern. They paddled a few strokes out, negotiating cross-waves. The canoe surged ahead in a powerful, seamless motion. The trees blurred. A second river fed in, its .with satisfaction, after the wrestling stretch.

"Challenge gives you character," Bacon shouted, against the wind.

"Character." Ray had found that repeating segments of conversation was a useful social tool. He was starting to relax. His shoulders felt warm. He felt in the peak of health. He took off his jacket. The misty rain felt cooling and healthy.

"Holy hell. Look up ahead ---" Bacon said. They had come around a bend, and ahead of them, the river narrowed, and the current picked up. "Popping like popcorn," Ray muttered to himself in between bounces, as they were caught in the maelstrom. This was the kind of challenge that got Ray high. The danger that made him feel alive. But they were jetting through currents swollen from record rains, and Ray was getting ever more inclined towards portaging around the Falls.

They careened around a few more curves of the river. As they shot out of one rapids the banks of the river rose in a gorge where the water surged with a speed a little too exhilarating. Probably over class 5 rapids, Ray speculated, as he balanced over an open hole he sensed, then saw behind them, after they had passed over the weak spot in the backwash. The rapids broadened as two other streams joined the river, forming a new series of whirlpools.

Ray's senses, alert from the start, went into overdrive. Again, Sage's words came to him. "I see death." A local swimming spot usually marked by a strip of sand on the river's edge was only visible by the top of a post with a life preserver hanging on it. Over the roar of the water and wind, Bacon yelled back to Ray, "Remember the plan." Ray did. They had gone over it thoroughly. Stay left. If at the strainer roots of a tree trapped on a boulder near the top of the Falls the current is too strong, cut hard right, make for shore.

The canoe rested lightly on the water. Under it, water simmered. Ray had never had such an acute experience of water about to boil over. As they were caught up in an overpowering swell, he shouted to Bacon, and at the same time, Bacon cut the water at a ninety-degree angle. The canoe veered, not so much that they caught the current broadside, but enough to head them diagonally toward the rocky bank of the stream.

They landed with a bump on the strip of beach. "A dent in a canoe is like a stamp in a passport," Bacon said, as they climbed out of the canoe. "Damn that current. Glad we made it out." He picked up a branch and cast it into the middle of the stream. It sucked under the water's surface, and then bobbed up in time to disappear precipitously over the lip of the falls. That was when Ray was aware of the fall's roar and the silence where they stood. The current they had been in looked like a lion's mane rearing up. Where the neck joined the head, not too far in front of them, the water ruffled like fur, and the falls cascaded down from the promontory of the lion's brow. A hungry lion.

§

COCKROACH

by Susan Tepper

June Klein's got no breasts but it don't bother me. Not even small humps. It don't matter.

"Want some?" I shove my bucket of movie popcorn at her.

"No thanks, William." She shakes her head and stares at the screen and sits up straighter in the seat. Her hair is short and black and stays back like bird wings when they're not flying.

It's after school and the movie is TOMCATS at the Bellaire. For October, it's still pretty hot outside. June Klein's got on shorts. In the dark I watch her round knees shine like two white softballs. I feel like pinching them. She got to pick which flick 'cause she asked me to go — in the lunch line at school.

I don't mind. A girl in the movie is already stripped to her underwear.

I rattle my popcorn. "Want some?"

June Klein shakes her head and her glasses slide down her nose. It's a shame about the popcorn. 'Cause she has a big box of Sno*Caps and I'd like a handful of those. A mouthful of corn, a mouthful of caps: the sweet with the salty.

"Huh!" I'm keeping one eye on this sexy blonde babe who's hot for the guy who's the star. Down down down her lips go, then land on his belly-button. Damn!

I push my legs over the top of the seat in front of me shoving more popcorn in my mouth. Keeping a watch on June Klein out of the corner of my eye. One by one she's eating those Sno*Caps. A couple of times she shakes the box — to see how much she's got left. That box has a good sound. Maybe I should go get a box of my own. But then I would miss what's coming next in TOMCATS. If she would just give me some, just a handful, it would solve that problem.

I turn my head and give June Klein a smile. She licks her lips and pops another Sno*Cap in her mouth. It's the same thing like with Sandy Sussman — the way she licked her lips before she kissed me. I don't think I'll be kissing June Klein.

"Cockroach," June Klein says.

"Huh?"

She points at the seat in front of her and stamps both her feet and starts to giggle. "Big fat cockroach."

"Whoa!" I say, throwing my head back.

We both stare at the roach moving slow across the top of the seat. That roach reminds me of a man crossing a mountain, a man out to discover gold in gold-rush country, then he loses his horse in an Indian raid and has to go the rest of the way on foot.

I hold a piece of popcorn close to the roach.

June Klein stabs me with her elbow. "Stop that!"

The roach stops in its tracks like it's listening to June Klein's command.

"Hey, that roach has ears!" I say.

"It doesn't seem to want your popcorn."

"Give it a Sno*Cap."

"I'm not wasting a Sno*Cap on some old cockroach," she says, quickly popping a couple into her mouth.

I take my feet off the seat in front of me, in case that roach should decide to do an about-face and start trucking in my direction. I decide that June Klein is some kind of pig. Only a pig wouldn't share; even if she hates popcorn. My old girlfriend, Sandy Sussman, she always shared. Sometimes I got M&M's and she would get the popcorn, and sometimes she got a Milkyway. Giant movie size. She'd put it on her lap and saw it in half with her nail file. Then she'd flip her long brown hair down one shoulder like a coon-tail, saying: "Herbal Essences keep me lookin' good."

I could have been the one she ended up with last summer.

Instead she took off with Tonka — this older kid from town with this tiger tattoo who supplies her weed.

June Klein is wiggling in the seat. She's twisting her head and looking around. With the hand not holding the Sno*Caps she's knocking at her hair. "Do you think there's any more roaches?" she says.

I'm not sure what to say to that.

The other guy starring in the movie, the one with yellow hair, is in the hospital. From cancer. One of his nuts just got cut off. He wants it back. He wants the other guy, the main star, to go find it. TOMCATS, I decide, is one sucko movie.

June Klein is staring in my face. So close, I can smell Sno*Caps on her breath.

"What if a roach jumps in my hair?" she says.

"What do you want from me? I can't control these roaches — they have a mind of their own." I point at the one still on top of the seat. "That one looks like the leader."

"That's ridiculous!"

"Shut-up, you kids!"

I poke June Klein on her arm. "Give that roach a Sno*Cap." She shakes one out of the box, looking at it in her palm.

"Here," I say, "give it to me."

But instead of passing it off on the roach, I lay it upside down on my tongue. It feels good: the hardness, the little white dots. I hold it there.

"You cheat!" she says.

"It's only one!" I roll it around my mouth then crush it between my teeth.

June Klein jumps up. "I want to go home. I hate this movie. Especially the sex scenes. If my dad finds out I'll get killed."

Shit, I'm thinking. Remembering how much Sandy Sussman loved the sex scenes. Sandy Sussman being one of the first girls in school to grow breasts. Probably right now she's off with that kid, Tonka. Sharing her candy and her breasts. Both of 'em laughing their asses off at TOMCATS. In some movie theater. Somewhere.

§

THE LANGUAGE OF LAUNDRY

Bird-of-paradise
thrives on our front balcony
as we move into the apartment
on Alameda Itu.

Centered on our new buffet,
your old family clock chimes
when you leave for work in the morning,
when you play golf on week-ends;
serenades each quarter hour
as Teresa and I clean, iron, cook,
a Westminster chorus
to our halting conversations.

Day after day
it carols me off to Portuguese class,
reminds me to shop on Rua Augusta
where every scent clutches at my throat:
raw meat from open butcher shops,
potions in farmacias,
cheap perfumes in the little boutiques.

At night, a recurring dream.

This time I wake,
leave you half asleep,
run through our dark apartment to the kitchen balcony,
laundry hanging from its ceiling,
knock on the maid's door
    Teresa, I dreamt I was suffocating.
    It was so real...

You hurry after me, tying your robe,
confused, wet shirts slapping your face.

- Pat Brodie

Mouse Trap

When I was very young, I was placed in charge of setting a mousetrap.
I baited it with cheese and set the trap by the back
legs of an old sofa.
Then, I laid on my belly, hands under my chin to
watch.

I think I must have fallen asleep, because
when I awoke the mouse was already in front of the
trap.
His little whiskers twittered as he slowly advanced,
sniffing the air.

To the mouse, I must have looked so big that I effec-
tively disappeared.
His tiny feet pushed him forward a tiny fraction of an
inch at a time.
Surely he would see the trap and run away.

But no.
He smelled the cheese and advanced on it after a long pause.
I closed my eyes.

I couldn't stand to watch, but I couldn't keep from watching.
The mouse looked around to see if there was any danger.
Then he nibbled a tiny piece of cheese.

He ate it thoroughly.
Then he took another nibble.
I began to think the trap was faulty and would not work
when SNAP!

The neck of the mouse was broken.
A little piece of cheese protruded from his v-shaped jaw.
He went without a twitch.

- Gary Lehmann

<u>WEATHER REPORT</u>

For a month it rained
lawsuit. Then
it snowed white on dark
retinal detachment,

an asphalt one-lane
getting narrower
as if elongated
by the pull of weather

suburbs
whited out
till there's nothing
on either side.

Cutbank, ditch
spine of a bucking horse
to drive on,
eyes shut tight

before the alarm
goes off
loud with silence
and forecast.

- Taylor Graham

THE VIEW FROM COYOTEVILLE

The South Fork sluices down
just out of hearing, a long history

having nothing to do with
No-Fishing-No-Swimming-No-
Gold-Panning a sign
the County put across
both abutments to the bridge.

You fish these waters by trespass,
beyond the discernment
of land-holders with their deeded
plats.

Nor do you heed the warnings
of a Surgeon General,
your lungs smoked out

while you ink-press hundreds
of printed pages,
backwoods anti-cosmopolitan
straight-talk.

But you're losing height
and breath in a slow
exhaling. Your ribs and eyes
tell a story

of the ways trout find,
a thin passage past your lines
downriver.

- Taylor Graham

THUNDER SNOW

Wild nights, wind-tossed days.

The crow flew from the rooftop
and disappeared

as snow began to sift down
such beauty

and you sat by the fire
reading old tragedies.

How can the gods forgive us?

The kettle gossiped
with the lid of the stove:

just listen to those drums
overhead!

Evening dimmed to blue, then
black, and still

it went on snowing, snow
with so many unpronounceable

names. By morning
a great stone

rolled against the door,
daylight

a lost promise.

- Taylor Graham

October Trio

The ash-gray heads
of goldenrod gone to seed
bob and swing.

Aspen trees applaud
with lemon-colored leaves.

Brittle blonde grasses
cleave and fall:
final bow.

- Clara Diebold

DENVER OMELET, SAUSAGE, HASH BROWNS

Damn, but I hate when she works late.
I could get carryout, or cook up
a burger and frozen fries, sip a solitary beer.
Wait – Andy's Diner is the answer:
Breakfast served all day – just the ticket.
Outside it's full dark – so early, these days.
Maybe I'll finish the book I've been reading forever.
But no, too much, too powerful, too glum
Soul-meandering: a total funk's
closing in: bills, job, the same old
same old, reality strangling delusions.
Time for desperate remedies.
Think, think hard about her: imagine
hair, voice, sweet gentle hands. Heaven be praised.

- John Hildebidle

I RECOGNIZED HIM AS A NEIGHBOR

Usually, the signal is considerable perturbation –
sparrow, squirrel, cats mutter anxiously.
Today it was oddly quiet. He took his ease
on a low branch, then swooped down
nearly to pavement level. A gull? I thought,
at first. But no, not white enough. Pigeon?
Far too large. Rising, he spread his tail –
THAT'S where the name comes from!
A red-tail surveying his estates, then
set off into the trees behind a nearby house.
This time even the brazen crows sounded an alarm.

- John Hildebidle

Sermon on Sun Worship

By Tomas O'Leary

That shimmering gestalt of basted bodies
Simmering naked in precise abandon
On hundreds of altars of colorful cloth
Spread with snug symmetry over the fine, white sand
Stunned me to ancient blood rite
Deep in the dark cells of my private being
As I trudged without nudeness aforethought
Down toward the blazing beach:
Hot from the dunes, ripe for the ocean, I
Utterly froze in the oven of my tracks
And gaped with an awe so witless
It transcended my erection!

The fresh, lovely corpses looked all of a unified field
In full flower of devourable languor
Under the maw of the Great Ra,
Whom I too would now have me completely;
I pealed off my suit and descended.

Near the fringe of that vast sacrificial grid,
The swirling millennia hazed me:
Preposterous lightly-tanned novice with ivory loin-stripe
Proposing to pass into trance among glazed devotees!
Some instinctual shyness restrained me
To panoramic scrutiny
Until my legs jerked with pure impulse to bear me,
A born-again ancient Egyptian,
Onto their close lanes of careful geometry.

There I wandered,
Most cautious for Ra's sake,
The banquet already in progress,
And studied with keen-eyed obliqueness
Each mound, scape and hummock
Of indolently flawless flesh.
That my heart was still beating (not barely,
But at twice its normal rate!)
Kept me walking, unsure of my place;
Faint liftings of eyebrow, however,
Odd twitchings of torso or limb
Assured me, though late to the service, I yet might join in.

I spread my own altar,
A terry towel covered with Einstein
Sticking his tongue out--
(Perhaps at Infinity,
Or some prosaic ex-lover)--
And lay belly-down on his moustache,
And offered my pale ass to Ra.

Ra's blistering teeth seized it swiftly
(Or so I imagined on two or three minutes'
Downpayment toward union forever)
While, licensed or pirate, all stations within me delivered
A piercing alert to seek shelter that instant--
Else lie there, and change for the worse.

Faith failed me:
I fled my rude altar,
I bared Einstein's tongue to the Sun God
And shot like an arrow into the blundering surf,
The wistful aroma of coconut high in my nostrils
Mixing with salt on my lips

To distract me with thoughts of this little Thai restaurant
Where you can pig out all day on exotic buffet
At reasonable prices

As I floated alone in the ocean,
The contrast so blissfully frigid
It quickly diminished my heat to some critical level
Conducive to euphoric stupor--
Till it struck me those purplish, five-headed creatures
Adrift several feet from my head,
Coldly watching me watch as they watched me,
So resembled two feet, they might just be!
I got the hell out.

The glorious corpses still simmered,
my foot landing hard here and there on a belly or limb;
though they grumbled, none rose from the dead.
I snatched up my Einstein at full stride
And never looked back.
I was out of the dunes in bare minutes,
My sporty blue Subaru swallowing shimmering asphalt
At hazardous speeds, my mind swimming
With hunger and thirst for some first-rate renewal,
All the way to the smog-throttled city
And straight to that Thai joint,
The promise of cold air, cool lighting, good food and a few drinks.

I parked, shut it off, took a deep breath, held it, and leapt
From my freon-fed fishbowl of conditioned air
Into the searing stench, the screaming of sirens,
My strained mind imploding with hyper-incitement to adjectival
riot
    and syntactic density
As I dreamed my legs into a trot.

Had I truly imagined transcending such over-indulgence?
Alas, I had laid my fat table;
Its main course would no longer release me,
Though I knew things could only get worse.

Not ten feet from that beckoning doorway
The parking lot split
Like a slug on a spit over hot coals:
Christ Jesus, an earthquake!

The fissure devoured me slowly,
Face-up for a last-ditch beseechment
To that microwave deity blindingly white in the brown sky;
All I asked was a three-hour extension
(I just had to get at that buffet)
Then I'd be a good pagan, jump back in my ditch roaring "Ra! Ra!"
But a voice--
(As of mountains and skyscrapers meeting in Denver
For head-on discussion of how they'd best serve one another
In the instance of global upheaval)--
Addressed me through holes in the ozone:

"O ye slave to infernal delusions of undulant matter:
Be still, and be damned!
All sensual refuge is dust in the eye of the Great Ra!"

Epilogue (The Sermon)

Before I could frame a response that might tie up those loose ends
Which can brand a meandering risk such as this "catastrophic,"
Before I could even quite grasp that the stage must be cleared now,
The dark prince Armageddon waltzed on with the grim Kali Yuga.

Ra should give a goddamn?

I could barely remember those corpses--
Decided to close with the earthquake,
Lie dead in my own poem.

Not an ending a poet dare live with--
Surely not a responsible poet!
Dare I blame the damned poem?

A poem is a self-contained system,
A delicate balance of passion and conscious restrain t--
Which this poem just ain't.
This poem blew up miles ago, under Ra, at the seashore;
"Too much," it kept screaming, while I said, "Oh hell, just a bit
more."
Till at last, richly bloated and bent on a sermon,
It squats on my brain like a blister.

And what of this Earth?
Earth abides like a poem, not a sermon.
A sermon might thrive as a gridwork of burgeoning sewers
Exploding haphazardly into some sluggish pool of discreet rumina-
tion;
A poem cannot do that and thrive.

I therefore surrender this poem to the Poetry Police.
All it lacks is official damnation.
All I ask is that they keep the pristine peace,
and label me very much wanted, dead or alive.

§

Comment ca va?

Meme's notes swing
up and down the stairs
the way my father dances
round and round my mother
at the Italian wedding.

Nothing remains of Latin
mass but the sonority
of the priest's incantations.

Your luminous surge
undoes the darkness,
unclothes my thoughts
Down pouring your light.

Stay, stay moon
held in place by a
mirage of images.
I study Latin by your
fractured light.

- Joanne Vyce

One Streetlight

one streetlight
one light
for empty corn field
lone car
rabbits
mice
opossums
live there

rusty old muffler
bits of blown tires
in the gravel

a light
in my eyes
as I drive past
then darkness
with just headlights to guide me

- Bonnie Pignatiello Leer

Menopausal Philosophy

I tell my daughter
I'm beginning menopause
"Oh, the first stage of dying,"
 she says
She's just read How We Die

Not the support I need
But wait
Deep inside I know
she's right
It's logical
The initial message of death

No wonder impatience has driven
me over the type-A edge
I don't have much time left
For traffic jams
Late friends
Return phone calls

Of course I have panic attacks
Meeting deadlines
Buying a new car
An outfit for next season

Explainable that I've cold-sweated
the ruin of every silk blouse
In business meetings
Key speaking
Playing bridge

Understandable that I can't sleep at
night because someday I won't wake up
Then crash on my office floor in the afternoon
Awaken with jolts
Naturally I stuff myself with rich foods
More sustenance means more life
Funeral food mentality

Perfect sense I cry over spilled milk
when I don't even like milk
Over LeAnn Rimes singing Blue
The paper arriving late
Babe the pig when he can't herd sheep

Justifiable that I flirt with banished vices
Cigarettes
Alcohol
Multiple men
It's all logical

I'm self-destructing
Why not surrender to the
natural process
Help it out a little
Forget about my husband
Daughters that set the moon
and raise the sun
Forthcoming grandchildren

- Ellaraine Lockie

middleair crosscry

still, (and stilled by)
one cry
that arcs forward
with its thousand thousand wakes.
onces
weighn weightlessly
smokeweavering in earth,
seapitched now and
ever,
interflown in fiery, seatraced keening.
soft, the crosscry,
archly,
greyly angry,
weaves its weathers
in ganged arrays of
singing,
interseathing between silken waters.
heat of fire in the blueprinted sea
flickers,
pressing the echoing light,
outcrying, from clay to breath.

- Eytan Fichman

Letters to Saïda

5 poems by Denis Emorine
translated from the French by Brian Cole

1
Behind us
such a wide sky
and you
comfortably hanging on to my arm.
I interrogate your amber eyes
the better to unwind my life.

One day
you will leave and I shall not know
where to find refuge
where I can better empty out my life.
Time will have clothed us in oblivion
even if I do not make up my mind.

We should not speed our pace
nor abolish the word
too soon ...

I know that dying exists

2
Death revolves slowly
in my head
when you are not there.

Perhaps I do not have the right
to throw myself
into your arms
to delete it with one stroke.

It has so many faces
and yet
I have the impression
that it knows only me.

I also call it folly
you know.

All these years will have been
for naught.
Folly is at the window
and beckons me.

I wander for ever
in the corridors of
my head
a loaded weapon
in my hand.

3
Why should we tell
all that there is between us?
Is it absolutely necessary
that our steps coincide?

Often it is useless to take
the most obvious path.

I have decided to go with you
until I can no longer.

How long will it take me
to erase myself from your life?

You will not like this question
no doubt
because the answer
does not belong to us.

But you know it.
There
yes, there
right next to my heart
which will have stopped beating.

4
One day
I shall retrace the course
of my life.

Without you
it is better so.

On that day
I shall abandon everything.
It will be difficult, you know!

I do not know if I shall have
the time to say
a few loving words.

You will be far away
and happy, I am sure.
You will feel nothing
I swear to you
scarcely a breath of wind
in your hair
a speck of dust in your eye
that you will have quickly
removed.

On that day
I shall die
on tiptoe

so as not to disturb you.

5
Saïda
I dare to mention your name.
I managed to write it.
Five letters
that I had
clasped
in my hand.

I have wasted too much time.
Why do I always keep looking
behind me?
I do not want to live too quickly
nor to jostle Time
that is
devouring me.

Saïda
at last I dare stroke your face
and keep the five petals
pressed
in my hand
without offending your name.

§

French Impression

My toes were kissed
on the steps of the Musée d'Orsay once.
It is hard for Americans
to impress the French.
They are so above it all.
Lofty, I presume.
But kissed my 10 toes were.
Each and every one.
Un, duex, trios,
Quattre, cinq, six,
Sept, huit, neuf, dix
In a moment of passion with
our 13 year old daughter observant.
Never to forget the
simple, funny loveliness of it all;
her father's love

- Kathy Horniak

You'll Be A Collyer Brothers Hermit!

Even then
my fingers were
stained with newspaper ink
gleaning information
for when I was
ready to speak.
And I thought-
the more news
I consumed
I could fill
some unarticulated
gap
and prove
there was something
behind all that
fat.
The stacks accumulated
in my room-
a garish, headlined
womb.
And when my father
evoked the brothers
at the side
of my bed
I retreated
under many covers
to bandage my
riotous head

- Doug Holder

Detroit For Sale, 1960s

In my mother's kitchen,
I eat chicken livers right off the
aluminum foil.

Outside the window:
"for sale" signs like cemetery stones,
from one house to the next.

Most of our old neighbors
are moving to a New Detroit in the suburbs.
My parents say we're not moving again…

I'm scared of the new German Shepherd, in chains,
in the garage next-door.

I'm not supposed to go outside alone.
I feel like a prisoner…
Just then, the dog in chains begins to howl…

- Barbara Bialick

Charon's Slow Day

It's no surprise to me that my bosses—
those who created the concept of work—
pick the days off most convenient for them,
even if others are plainly left behind.
But there are still opportunities
when the people aren't lined up,
hoping their forms are in proper order
to get across, screaming when they're not,
or even if they are, never figuring out why I'm so quiet.

During these times, the guardians to both sides
seem to keep at bay, as if afraid of their own wards.
Once in a while, I'll sneak a skull
under my robe, despite policy insisting
that the Lost and Found never be emptied.
My son can use them as soldiers' caps
for a game of One True Army,
and I'm the Cool Dad for a while longer.

Most in line would be surprised
to find I have eyes. I'm always looking down,
leaning back only when there's a lull.
I don't see well, but with the right squint,
the view looks like shore, not bone;
and I am reminded of every beach front
I have never seen, my mind discarding them
before improbability ever set in.
I only need to walk the length of my oar
from end to end as it rests on the side,
and it is accomplished. I believe for a while
that all this has nothing to do with me.

- Chad Parenteau

Trees in December

The trees are standing bare
Unassumingly aware
There's a perched owl staring into the mind
Of a young girl turning

There's a wheelbarrow
Sitting with its heart wide open
Pointing to the south
There's a wing up above
It's moving with Decembers prelude of love

And the sky is wide open

There's an old house up upon the hill
It's been empty ever since I can remember
The river runs along the side
And I think that's where I'd hide if I had to
That's where I'd hide

And the sky is wide open

Starkness climbing up a wall
Each vine symbolizing all the sides now
I wonder what is mine
And what belongs to the sign of the season
What belongs to the sign

And the sky is wide open

When I look back I want to remember
The defining days
And the trees in December
The trees in December

- Jennifer Matthews

untitled by John Mercui Dooley

if though and ink with
doesn't lost and room
unadorned "beautiful"
for example hang
living pieces elements
so glue print.

print ink and thing ink
doesn't beautiful lost
hang unadorned
elements for example
print living.

living in tricky ink
dust and thing a what
large positive ink
horizontal lost shapes
for example.

- John Mercui Dooley

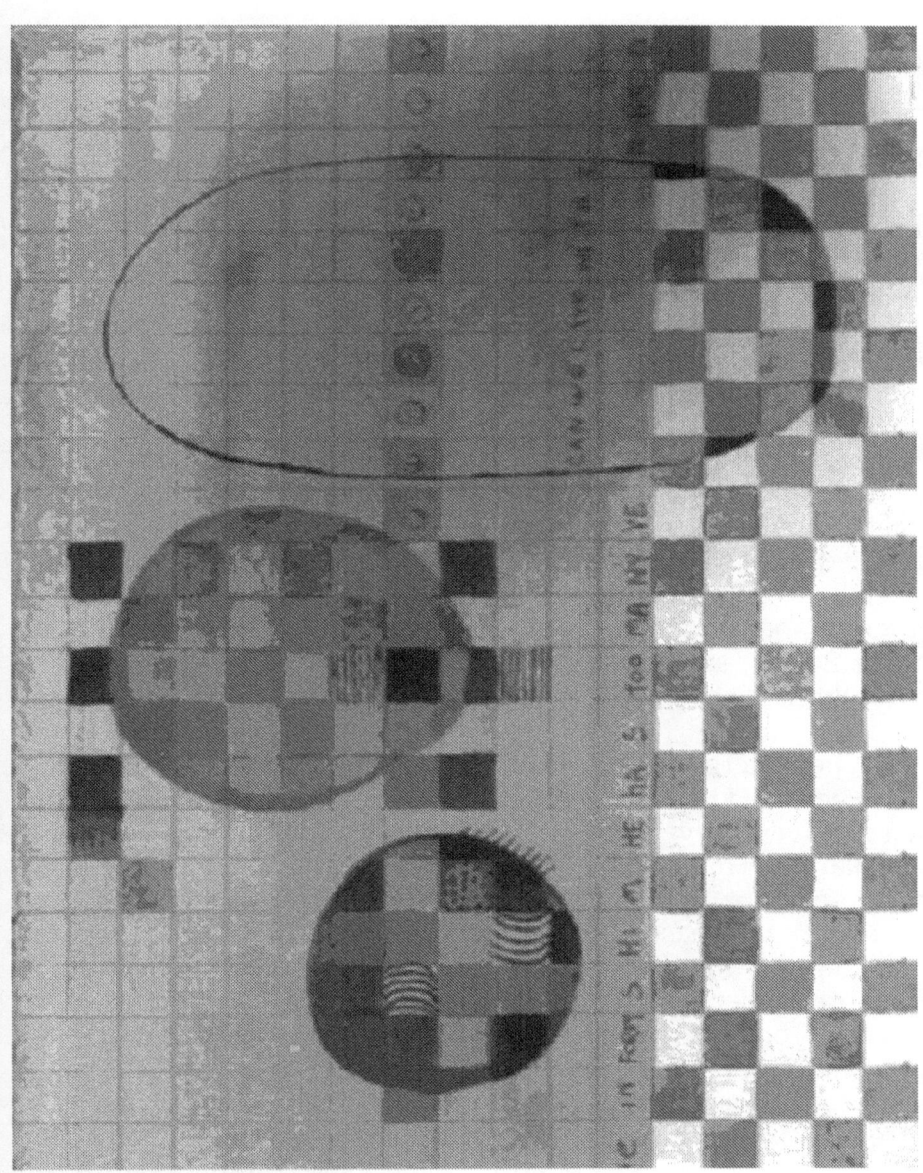

The art of Irene Koronas

ellipse and parabola
"a zero at infinity" Charles Seife

By Irene Koronas

Do all living shapes contain infinity? If so, then, does infinity shape all matter. From a human view point, infinity seems a perfect round shape (ellipse) and the world may be imagined as a round shape. Is all matter a point of view and it's shape or form surmised as a particular shape or form from 'that' point of view? 'That,' being the point of view of the viewer. The ellipse is a definition of what may be perceived as a round shape. The parabola is the projection of an energy from the position of the ellipse, from a movement away from the ellipse, a different angle, same position, different vantage point, an energy field released from the shape, (it's shape?) As applied to the life form; when I stand, look at a rose, I think I am seeing a rose, when I move ever so slightly I see the rose from another perspective; the shadows change, and the shape of the rose changes. Is it the same rose? What influence does the rose's energy have on the viewer?

When energy is contained it can explode or if contained by degrees (released by degrees) that same energy can remain contained forever. Forever meaning the life of the objects, shapes, forms, plants, animal and living matter. I use the words shape and form to represent all that contains energy, which is everything. When energy is released by degrees or released until all energy merges, with, or into infinity, then that energy effects and merges with all other energy in the atmosphere. One can say one energy is positive and one energy is negative. But energy is energy. It becomes a matter of the position taken by thinkers as to how the energy is used. Some energy is perceived as negative and some energy is seen as positive. Again energy is energy. One being that which contains energy. Contained energy can be a self contained attitude, self, meaning, any living form, even though all living forms emit energy, it is the parabola, the deliberate position taken by human motivation, the projection of one's energy or an energy which captures and contains or projects, in this case projected, as in parabola, that interests me. Of course, a flower can change it's position, but, the position changes because of the direct influence of the sun. Is it possible, for direct influences, to come from the infinite position or a position that is moveable because of the direct influence of the infinite? The infinite as defined by zero.

Coming from the point of human behavior, I suggest, projecting one's energy can influence all energy, all living matter. This is true in both a positive , negative or the between position of neither, nor. I also suggest, it is the zero, the position of infinity which energizes and sustains our universe. The zero as a symbol of the infinite or the nothingness of explanation of nothing. I do not consider it a number but the beginning of numbering, the before of numbering. It is our relationship with zero, with definitions of infinity. It is within our numbering or human position which clashes and resists infinity. Zero is not an absolute position. This is a position of movement, of investigation, of the self in relationship with all other matter. An absolute is, nothing is certain, nothing is permanent, everything seems to die. Another absolute is, there is zero evidence to prove how existence began and when it will end, there are only suppositions, and evidence may point to a particular position, theory, but not an absolute position or theory. The infinite is a position that can be moved or moves constantly. Infinity sustains all forms of life and all forms of life move. The negative energy, the static energy, can be used for whatever the positioner deems its' use. Negative energy is only that energy which we perceive as destructive but in fact is simply energy that causes a reaction, that effects matter in an adverse way but it cannot destroy, in an absolute sense, it only effects. Our perception of positive energy is the same, if effects in ways that are perceived as good or sustainable but again it is merely energy, energy connected to energy, a tangent.

zero being nothing, contains all energy, whatever energy may be defined as. infinity always being nothing, because we cannot contain infinity or is infinity contained within what I previously talked about, the form as matter. All other numbers or forms are added to or subtracted, divided like the stuff of math, the stuff of a material life. We think we are adding to our life. We think we are subtracting from our life. We are only changing our position and seeing a longer perspective. The self help programs, help us to change our position, our reaction to the effects of a position, an attitude about who we are and what we can and cannot do or what we can except about ourselves and from the influences of the outside world. All spiritual representations can lead us to make a shift in who we think we are. We have choices. Can we live as zero, can we live with zero? How do we want to influence our surroundings?

§

EDDIE AND NELLIE
a Book Report

By Jim Woods

It's a small book, a boy-sized book, measuring four and a half inches by six and three-quarters. It's hard bound, as books were in those days, in reddish-brown Buckram cloth, embossed on the front with black trim and corner scrolls, but no words, no title. The spine, decorated in the same black décor but also including several patches of faux gold, announces the title, Frank in the Woods, one of the Frank and Archie Series by the publisher, Porter & Coates.

Inside though, we find that Porter & Coates, of Philadelphia, apparently owns, or did own, a subsidiary imprint house in Cincinnati, Ohio, R.W. Carroll & Co., and that is the actual print source for Frank in the Woods. The book is "registered"—the word "copyright" apparently not in use—in the year of its publication, 1865.

The book enjoyed staying power. The front endpaper is personally dedicated in scratchy blue ink hand script: "Presented to Eddie By Nellie On His 14th Birthday Oct 20th 1881." Sixteen years after publication the book is still being purchased for young male readers in the family.

But what family? There is no surname, only the given names of Eddie and Nellie. And who is Eddie to Nellie? Best guess: brother and sister. The inscription lacks the endearment that would have been included had the gift been from a favorite aunt or even Eddie's Mother, and had the book been from one of those, the familiarity of the first name of the giver would not have been so prominent. The adolescent penmanship testifies that the gift came from another juvenile. Since Eddie has just reached the manly age of fourteen, it's safe and logical to assume the gift was not from a girlfriend. No, the giver was Eddie's sister who was careful to not display any public affection for her brother, but she did present him a favorite book.

The author is one Harry Castlemon, apparently a prolific writer whose YA works include multiple titles in The Gun-Boat Series; The Go-Ahead Series; and The Rocky Mountain Series. All of these books are individually cover priced at $1.25 or $1.50 and all are (were) available in boxed sets. For instance, six volumes of The Gun Boat Series were available "in a neat box" for $7.50. Three volumes comprise the other two series, and they too come "in a neat box" for $4.50 or $3.75. There is no price break or premium for buying by the boxed set, but neither is there a charge for the "neat box" that contains the set. Nellie thought well enough of Eddie to give him a single volume, but not enough to spring for the complete set.

Castlemon utilizes the Authorial Intrusion technique as he sets the scene in the opening pages, reminding the reader of who the characters are, making the assumption that the reader has a history with his characters:

"Our scene opens in the swamp that stretches for miles north of Lawrence [Maine] . . . . A rude hut . . . ready to receive beneath its friendly shelter four boys, whom you could easily recognize as our old friends of the sailing and fishing frolics described in "The Young Naturalist." We left them, after a hard day's work at fox-hunting. . . . To enable the reader to understand how we come to find them here in the woods, twenty miles from any human habitation, we must conduct him [the reader] back to Lawrence, and relate a few incidents with which he [the reader] is not acquainted."

He does so again at the conclusion, making the boys' literary adventure into a serial similar to the genre that later intrigued movie-going youngsters, and which has passed into cinematic history just as Castlemon's literary serial also has become passé.

The author's narrative, as might be expected for the times, is worded in formal English, but surprisingly the four young boys speak to one another in the same precise phrasing. The author perhaps sees his juvenile characters as younger versions of himself, or the way he would like to see the young people of his day conduct themselves. Harry, the boy character, not Harry the author, addresses his companions:

"Now, boys, this is the kind of life I enjoy. Doesn't it make a fellow feel comfortable, to lie here and listen to the storm, and know that he is securely sheltered? For my part, I don't see how a person can live cooped up in a city all his life."

Note that the four boys' ages are not actually delineated in the story, but before embarking on their adventure, Frank and Archie agreed that they required permission from "Aunt Mary," and then cajoled that permission from her, indicating that these are indeed young boys, possibly early teenagers. The other two boys, Harry and George, later are recorded as having obtained their parents' permission to join their cohorts. If parent or guardian approval was required, and heeded, then these four are not young men but young boys.

However, the boys are remarkably self sufficient and proficient in woodcraft. Perhaps that's indicative of not just boys but of all the people of the time. This stalwart quartet treks twenty miles a day over wilderness country, in a storm, then rises eagerly the following morning, washes their faces in snow, and cooks a camp breakfast. No fast food breakfast biscuit sandwiches here!

The boys reach the remote cabin of the old hunter, "Uncle Joe." Just whose uncle is not specified; perhaps not a real relation as much as simply everyone's uncle. But another man shares the cabin at the moment, Uncle Joe's brother, Dick, who is shown to be hero and mentor to the boys. Not an athlete on America's team; not a racecar driver; not a hip-swinging, electric guitar banging rock star, but an Indian-fighting, hunting and trapping superman of the wilds:

"He was a fine specimen of a North American trapper, fully six feet in height, with a frame that seemed capable of enduring any amount of fatigue. Thirty years among savage beasts, and still more savage men, had brought him in contact with almost every variety of danger. He had . . . taken on more than one rough-and-tumble fight with Rocky Mountain grizzlies; was very expert with the rifle; could throw a tomahawk with all the skill of an Indian; and could lasso and ride the wildest horse that ever roamed the prairie."

The stellar resume of Dick the wilderness hero, goes on in great detail to describe more of his exploits, It's no wonder that Frank and his companions within the pages, and the newly-turned four-teen-year-old Eddie to whom Nellie presented the hard-bound adventure, it can be assumed, held Dick in such high regard. But the trapper idols did not live so poorly, at least in Harry Castlemon's stories. Another member of the trapper team is part of the cabin crew as well:

"Bob, who was one of the hired men, began to bustle about, and, after hanging the tea kettle over the fire, he drew out a pine table, and covered it with a snow-white cloth, and dishes which shone in the fire-light in a manner that would have delighted a new England housewife. Then came ham and eggs, which, with the coffee, were cooked in the fireplace, wheat bread, honey, and fresh butter and milk."

This passage, if in today's literature, would carry a strong implication of homosexuality—multiple men living together under the same roof, remote from civilization, with at least one member of the group defined by feminine traits and work assignment. Castlemon does not overtly pursue that notion, but it would carry such implication in the modern-day permissive world. Whether Castlemon intended such a veiled implication is up to the reader, and most likely would not have presented such meaning to the juveniles to whom his stories are directed. If the author did indeed intend social commentary, political correctness had not affected his wilderness paradise. Dick's dog leads the way when he alerts the cabin to possible danger with his barking and growling:

" 'Injuns ag'in, by all that's miserable,' . . . 'Come back here, dog,' said Dick. 'I don't blame you, 'cause they are a mean, thievin' race. The animal understands their natur' as well as I do,' he continued . . . 'Me and him war [were] brought up to hate Injuns, an' we believe in makin' war on 'em wherever we find 'em. It's a mighty wonder that they don't steal Joe out of house an' home.' "

Hate, racial intolerance and possibly libel— any editor today would blue-line such author's work out before publication. And if the editor passed it, the publisher's legal squad surely would prevail and have the offending copy removed, particularly in a young adult book that would be sure to be banned from the school library. Today's schoolboy, today's Eddie, must be protected from such human thought.

A pair of local Indians with whom Uncle Joe was friendly, entered the cabin and prepared to sleep on the floor in front of the fire, much to the dismay of Dick who continued denigrating the Indians as thieves and rascals. The following morning with the Indians gone early, Dick may be proven right; some fox traps are missing from inventory and of course Dick blames the loss on the two Indians. The four boys are excited over the grand adventure, trailing the Indians to retrieve their property, lead by Dick the Indian fighter.

The young boys' precise command of language shows up again in a passage following Dick's notice to them that the Indians were too far ahead, and they would have to run in order to catch up to them. Dick challenged the boys to keep up with him.

"We should not care about running a race with you," answered George; "but if you will hold this gait, we will agree to keep up with you."

It's difficult to imagine middle teen boys of today speaking so, and one must wonder if indeed that similar aged boys of the era of this story were so precise in thought and expression.

As for Mountain Man Dick, had he lived in present day, surely would be in social, literary and possibly legal troubles when, after catching the Indians and recovering the boys' traps, laid a severe tongue lashing on the pair and called them "painted niggers." And he didn't stop there with his abusive political incorrectness. Back at the cabin Dick regaled the boys with trapping stories that led to a tale about his favored and heirloom bear trap. It seems the coveted item of trapping equipment was stolen from time to time but once was purloined by "a yaller-hided Mexikin Greaser."

To his credit, though, Dick had a talent for enduring in the wilderness and instructed the boys in woodcraft. That education for the young characters in the story no doubt empowered the young readers of the tale as well, and fourteen-year old Eddie might well have looked upon the birthday gift book as his very own adventure survival manual. Sister Nellie had given him so much more than a mere book.

Each of the twenty chapters starts with an elaborately scrolled — actually not scroll but vines and blossoms — initial letter that's seven lines high, and since the openings are not always the same word, that initial letter scrollwork varies in design, lending a noticeable artistic flair to the look of the book.

That fancy artwork initial lettering is not the only graphic treatment in the book. There are two full-page illustrations, printed one side on glossy photographic-weight paper decidedly different from the texture of the text stock, much as one of our modern-day books would treat photographs interspersed between text pages. These ink sketches are not the work of a single artist, or at least that artist does not get personal credit, but the style does indicate that the same artist created both pieces of work. The drawings are identified by the corporate name of the art house, Milburn & Mallory, but there is no frontispiece credit line for Milburn & Mallory such as we sometimes see today for contributing artists and photographers.

Oddly enough, both drawings depict a moose. In the first, young Frank is under attack by a wounded rogue mature moose and in the later one, the boys have broken a young moose to harness, making the animal their sled horse. Artistically, the wise old experienced moose that attacked Frank looks very much like the young, and presumably more modestly antlered, moose trained to harness. An insignificant conclusion could be reached that the artist never saw a real moose.

The boys' adventures continue to include encounters with wolves, foxes, beavers, a painter [panther] and a grizzly bear, as well as the harsh winter weather, all in the company and under the guidance of mountain-man Dick. It's easy to assume young male readers of the era sharing in these literary adventures with author Castlemon's intrepid cast.

And if Castlemon's four boy character's story were not enough, those boys and the readers are treated to more of Dick's exploits back at the cozy cabin as the mountaineer storyteller regales the boys with more of his exploits in the wilderness. But obviously Frank, Archie, Harry and George are simply straw men to whom the tales seemingly are directed when the real audience is the young reader Eddie and his kind.

The adventure coming to a close, the boys head for home, each carrying his own remembrance of their escapades, and author Castlemon adds his summation as if to remind the reader as well.

There was no danger that the boys would soon forget the wild scenes through which they had passed during their short sojourn in the woods. Each had something to remind him of some exciting hunt which he had gone through. Frank thought of his desperate struggle with the buck, during which he had received scars that would go with him through life. Harry remembered his adventure with the wolves. George shivered as he thought of his cold bath in the pond. And Archie, in imagination, was again in pursuit of the black fox.

The episode closes with the boys in dialogue with one another, embellishing their tales, but the intrusive Harry Castlemon has the last word:

"Here we will leave them, only to introduce them again in other and more stirring scenes on the Western Prairies."

For this reviewer, it's a broad leap from Maine to the Western Prairies, but author Castlemon is capable of broad leaps, geographically and literarily. Subsequent titles in the series have Frank placed not only on the prairie but also on the Mississippi River and in the Rocky Mountains. Obviously the young character is well traveled.

However, there is a charm to the stories, and undoubtedly they thrilled the boys of the era to whom they were directed. This was a time before motion pictures, before television, text-messaging and interactive adventure games at the arcade. They also are very substantial books, several quality grades above the dime novels that preceded them. As noted, the books are small, for smaller hands, but big in content to feed big imaginations.

Actually, the book really isn't physically so small. At 250 pages and between 50,000 and 55,000 words, it qualifies as novel by today's word-count standards. Eddie could have done a lot worse in fourteenth birthday presents than to receive yet another volume of Frank and Archies' epic adventures, and was lucky indeed to have Nellie in his life, whoever she is, making his participation in those adventures possible.

§

October Run in Danehy Park

By Sarah Merrow

The bathhouse mural at the entrance announces "Danehy Days" as I jog past in a cold rain. In knee-banging anticipation of a mindless trip down recycled glass paths, I'm full of hope - for relief from malaise, for the warmth of exercise, for a whiff of mountains - hoping respiration and inspiration will combine, tossed with the rhythm of running.

Elevated above the neighborhood, ringed by willows ringed by beds of stone, it's a dump. That is, it was a dump, but at present, it's an urban oasis. The grass is flooded today along perimeter walkways; local footballers are bawling in their corner, bumping helmets, and making mud and noise like steers on a cattle drive. I reach the baseball field where the path's underwater, and climb the back-stop's chain-link to stay on track, looking down at mini ripples whipped by the wind. From my height, I wonder how deep? Reflecting an ironclad sky, they might conceal a drowning. And on, hugging the park-edge past vacant soccer goals where it's too wet for kids, but not the sparrows holed up in the fence. One bird, then forty, dart from their aluminum diamonds into tossing heads of Queen Anne's lace, brown-cupped and brittle with seed in late October. Drizzle prickles take the same angle, with the same urgency, into the open mouth of my jacket. Happy at last, glasses fogged, all knees and neck, hot inside, numb out. Breathe, relax into the bounce, keep going.. There's a knot of Latinos up ahead where walks intersect, stalling around a makeshift tent that harbors tee shirts for THE WARRIORS. Huddled in sweat suits, out of their element. One whistles a low warning - gringa coming through - and I tight my way through the group, hearing their sparrow-spanish reform behind me, the way a flock of birds circles back around when you've advanced too far into their territory. I take the low road now, lined by matted grasses once wavy with sunlight. To prolong my

return to alpha gate, I walk. The mall's off to the left, hilltop fields
on my right, and ahead, picnic grounds with no sport today but ta-
ble-sailing. Beyond, thirsty willows drink up the run-off, and shield
the condos lining this land from prying eyes.

Did they think we wouldn't look among the weeds, willows,
and hills of their constructed garden for its machinery? Here's the
pump. I would have seen it at the outset had I run widdershins.
Had I first taken the narrower path. Shackled, enclosed in ubiqui-
tous clank-link, ON light a-blink, painted handles at rest, it sits atop
a slab atop the biggest septic system in town, Danehy's forbearer,
the Sherman Street dump. Monitoring its underworld for the sake
of athletes, tots, neighbors, and loiterers, it drains the whole place.
A knobby thing of blue-gray arms outstretched in a cage.

§

Photo by
Steve Glines

The Guilty One

The christ of the corn has risen
straw arms outstretched. Crows
dot the parched earth, peck for kernels
at his feet. Eyes of coal hot
in the dry sun. No smell of rain
in sight. Some demon spits dust
into a wind of cracked leather. Feathers
fall from some of the birds, bare
patches of taut flesh exposed, claws pierce
the arms of the scarecrow. Three
children race, shattering dry clods
of sullen soil, a wrenching of tired
wings, one crow does not fly. It
sits perched on the crown

of christ watching as the three
come close. Black dots for eyes. One
child pauses, swallows, bends to
grasp a stone and casts it into the air.

The christ of the corn is still. The crow
shudders at the feet of straw. One
child, the caster of stones, kneels
to place his hand on the bird. His
heart beats in a vacuum and the noise
of it echoes in his ears. He looks
up at the eyes of the scarecrow. The others
stand by him. He is alone. The
second child

takes out a cigarette, lights
a match. He touches it to the arm
of the scarecrow. Fire
runs up the arm of the strawman, burns
into the sockets of the eyes. The third
child does

nothing.

- Marc D. Goldfiner

Amorphophallus Rivieri

He is there behind branches in the wood
his hands plant shoots, grafts from the warrior snake
the garden variety one that could
see eggs, sugar, flour mixed into a cake
and announce sweetly it was made from scratch
just for birth day, knock it down for the dog
hissing, "not enough for another batch"
he plants past roots, buries old bulbs in fog
black pupils set in some blue eyed sea link
of powerful men grown in the self love
of real war, stomping the sad part; a wink
of "get over it real men rise above
snakes, cakes that fall..." fathers that hit me...
fully grown, I bloom like a corpse lily

- Stephen Morse, Minnesota

Why some stay alive:

soap less, warm baths of olive oil and milk
in a clean, white tub.

twenty matches for twenty cigarettes.
unordered coffee with a splash of un-asked-for bourbon
at Jozefina's on a
cold colorless Saturday morning.

slight smile from someone you almost know
and who almost knows you,
like a seed about to shoot.

a rosewood rosary blessed in Rome.

that picture of you,
half-facing the camera,
that I look for every so often,
but cannot find,
and is there.
There it is.

A chestnut, for inspiration,
puffy hear halved.

- Francis LeMoine

Trophy

Poetry is a love line, laugh line, blood line;
a blotted line that never quite dries.
It is a drop of aged wine, only a drop,
not spilled, a fine taste that lingers.
A shot glass emptied to relieve the angst
when no thoughts pool on teeming dormant paper.

Poetry is a vault of hoarded thoughts.
When it finally squeaks open on stubborn hinges,
you fish blindly in the depths.
Surprise ! Only a starving moth staggers out to expire.
Its death scene lasts the whole third act,
seen with new clarity under a magnifying glass.

You sit on a weathered Windsor rocker.
You scan your microfiche dreams,
then cast your line and troll the clouds.
Unseen creatures nibble the bait until the hook is clean.
With breath as a lure, your rod bends double.
What races below churns the surface.
The turbulence calms in the sunset's spreading net.
You reel in your trophy poem.

- Harris Gardner

Tractor In Field

The old tractor dreams in a field of snow. The tires
are flat & cracked, fenders red with rust, elderly
flywheel locked tight. It hasn't had a drink in years,
though the rain washed over the rusty steel saddle
where no one ever sits.

- Eric Greinke

Wild Strawberries

Coming across them
Unexpectedly, as
A child, they
Taste as fresh
As red. Hard
To collect enough
To bring home
For jam, so we
Eat them while we can.

- Eric Greinke

14 Stones, 76 Metaphysical Excursions, 6 Years
after Harold Weston

14 stones
the chosen
scree

6 years in
the artist's
studio
reifying
the image

layering
excursions
one upon another

all those imagining
nights becoming
Tibetan Dawns off
the coast of Maine

- Alan Catlin

Options:

1.

vocal or gestural invitation
or warning

the will to attack
in whatever form
with whatever implement
or not

or as if dead
or at complete peace

2.

claimers
or owners (known by some as
the inevitably immoral)
touch in whatever capacity
the claimed

of and for
energy "x" the body

a conduit: nerves
signal action reaction

example:

a petted Persian purrs

or

with the raising
of a rolled Wall Street Journal
a yelled-at Pekepoo
clenches his/her mouth
for pissing on the floor

example:

during a bout of
heavy-petting, a horny
lover bites his/her lover's
double chin

or

when a lightening bolt strikes
earth, the bald
monk continues his stroll

- Kevin McLellan

PLEIADES RISING

Tonight
I sit alone
an old zen poet,
listening to his breath,
and watching midnight stars
rising above November trees
and her Maxwell Parrish eyes
in my memory.

The first time I saw her, I stopped.
Don't ask me why, I can't explain
total strangers on a cold afternoon
standing among Cadillacs
in a January rain.

The second time, by accident
we met again,
it was the same as before,
my heart lay pulsing on the floor,
she and I, two tourists
on a mountaintop in North Carolina
during an August
thunder and lightning storm.

And then one day - in Hong Kong
her lips met mine -
white clouds - her perfume,
butterflies filled the universe
the Chinese Conservatory Orchestra
played around us
marching through the room.
Firecrackers exploded!
Gung Fu warriors
lifted the Cosmic Dragon
in His dance to the beating drum,
the beating drum

Tonight,
I sit alone,
an old zen poet
listening to his breath
watching these midnight stars
rising above November trees
and her Maxwell Parrish eyes
forever in my memory.

- Howard Lee Kilby

Cybermorphing Forsythias

2 bright yellow forsythias glow
in the engaging Spring sun
reminding me of the bush
I read Tolstoi by 45yrs ago

behind me, now on cd
Sinatra conducts Alec Wilder
who delighted me at 17
in West Lynn, before I fled to

Beacon Hill, then Cambridge,
beating the Vietnam War draft
forever changing my life,
its continual crises bridging

those & these newest
antiwar days in this poem
I'm writing on a laptop
in an upscale Boston suburb,

cybermorphing forsythias
into my living brain-coral.

- Bill Costley

STRICT OBJECTIVITY

By John Hildebidle

It's important you know that, of my two surviving children, one (the elder) is a biological son, the other is an adopted daughter. I'm always happy to accept compliments about either. But, since I think my son bears a remarkable resemblance to me and my father, I do blush just a bit when someone labels him handsome. But with my daughter, it's a different matter entirely.

She and I went to a funeral together the other day, and probably a dozen people or so who hadn't seen her recently (she's been away at college) made a point of declaring she was "beautiful" (or gorgeous or stunning or a synonym). I was hardly disposed to disagree, and I realized I could just bask in the admiration she received, since it was (biologically speaking) none of my doing. She is, as it happens, a fine loving young person, and I'll take some credit for that. But only some.

It is, I think, one of the hidden or at least unspoken advantages of adoption – you can accept any compliment that is launched toward the adopted child for his/her looks, without any taint of egotism on your part. I call that true liberation.

But there is as well a sadness. My daughter was left on a doorstep as an infant (in a place where she was certain to be found and cared for and probably adopted by an American family). I am haunted – literally – by the thought of her mother (don't expect me to explain why I am certain it was her mother), having put down the basket in which the child, warmly wrapped and well-dressed, lay, walked away, never to see her again. Since I am all too aware of the peculiar and rich nature of the father-daughter bond, it is odd that I don't think I've ever thought about her biological father at all.

But I do find myself, not infrequently, looking at my daughter in amazement – how could I possibly have earned this? And then comes the sadness – her biological parents don't know the astonishing person she's grown into. I don't know, of course, what moved them -- irresponsibility? Desperation? Some inexplicable variety of human infifference? – to abandon her. But I do know, and grieve for, just how much they've missed.

§

a letter to Doug Holder from Jared Smith
A Poet in the 70's -in Greenwich Village- in love with life...

By Jared Smith

You sank me into memories. I don't know how one could write an essay of what life was like in The Village in the 70s...or what my life was like. I was riding a drunken comet...a young man who was making it into the big leagues almost and was able to hang out with and be tolerated by the big boys. And they were billboard big, and I worshipped them and wanted to be able to think like they did and speak as they did, but at the same time I had to figure out how to start to make a living and how to get as many girls as I could into bed and do as many other crazy things as I could.

My writing took off while I was still in graduate school at NYU...30 poems published in literary magazines, some good and some bad in my first year...as many as 120 publications in 12 months only four years later. William Packard invited me to join the screening committee of The New York Quarterly, and later the Board of Directors. Don Lev invited me to be a Guest Columnist on Home Planet News. Harry Smith pegged me as the next big thing, and Walter James Miller had me on his NPR author-interview show twice. I drank and cried with Gregory Corso, watched Allen Ginsberg wander around The Eighth Street Book Shop ("Where Wise Men Shop"), a hulking heavy man bent over with a canvas bag draped over his shoulder, in which he carried an American Express Card machine and copies of his books so people could buy them from him on credit, and I mused about how he looked like a cave man, but he really could howl. I thought nothing of taking multi-hour bus trips to hear poets like Robert Bly read when they blew into New Jersey or wherever else—he reading to my girl and me and three others with his bright serape flailing across his shoulders until he kissed my girl and she fainted dead away at his feet. We wrote back and forth for years afterwards about dragon smoke and other things. And Albert Goldbarth, who like me as years went by, turned into science and technology as well as poetry. Harry Smith, my first publisher, with Lloyd van Brunt and Sydney Bernard and Tom Tolnay, equaling the mighty Smith Press. Talking with Bill Packard in his apartment surrounded by enormous plastic garbage cans—industrial size—which filled his living room and served as waste paper baskets, thinking up personal notices to run in the end pages of NYQ—nasty digs at the lady poets he loved to publish and really didn't want to feel close to. Writing story-boards for almost-produced PBS films on the works of Susan Fromberg Schaeffer, Charles Bukowski, and Packard's Ty Cobb Poem...and how I lost that contract because they decided they'd only do those if I could deliver Kurt Vonnegut as well, and I didn't know how to get to him. A woman from the suburbs who ate my soul because I couldn't burn it bright enough, and another who saved it by throwing water in my face until I choked. Coordinating readings at The Basement Coffee Shop and The Café Feenjon. Having Jerome Rothenberg attend three of my readings in a row and being too stunned to ever talk to him because his Banging On The Pumpkin had just come out, and I was still a kid and wouldn't know what to say to him. And Menke Katz—no man who knew Menke or his writing could ever forget the man, nor could any woman, for other reasons which the women could tell you of. His Burning Village remains an incredible epic, and all of his work haunts me. The names come back in different contexts too...Don Lev was my best friend's roommate, and a good friend of mine as well. I remember him starting up with Enid Dame when they first met each other. Galway Kinnell...well, we're going to 1963 for this...but him reading from What A Kingdom It Was when that first came out, long before Body Rags and The Book of Nightmares. He had always wanted to spend time on Cape Cod when he was younger, and couldn't afford to...so one winter when the vacation homes were all boarded up, he dug up through the floor of one. He was a fighter then too: he marched for civil rights in the south and had to be busted out of jail by calling the Dean's office at NYU's School of Continuing Education. He never told me this, but it was true. It was just a time to live. I resided for a year at the top of Judson Church, in the room Edwin Arlington Robinson lived in, and above a myriad of tunnels that connected the New York underground and its radicals so that they could slip from building to building without coming up. And I lived at the corner of West 12th Street and West 4th—where parallel lines come together in infinity. An essay could not be written of infinity...of the open doorways between apartments where film-makers from Paris and poets from Canada and artists from wherever came through and stayed a week and left and were replaced by others without the apartments ever changing hands...a building that had first opened in the 1800s as a hotel for whaling men in for a few days from sea. Never enough to eat, but never hungry because you could always find someone with something and it was an endless circle of energy.

And then I had to leave for a while, and was relocated to the Midwest where I kept writing, but more and more had to devote my creative hours to technology research and business education while raising a family. Would you believe, I—with only my two degrees in literature--ended up assisting in the development of international energy policy, consulted with most of the Fortune 500 and with McGraw-Hill and The New York Merc and several universities, worked with various government agencies, finally advising several White House Commissions on security and emergency response under Clinton, and then landing a major Defense Department research contract and working on that with a team of scientists, before serving as a Special Appointee to Argonne National Laboratory and assisting in various critical infrastructure studies relating to energy and telecommunications. Literature must be a way of thinking in unique ways about a lot of things that are worth a lot of money to other people, I guess. Too bad more people don't read.

Broke free again in 2000 at the age of 49, and I've been writing fulltime ever since. But you can't put all that into an essay, and it doesn't scan, and people don't see how the one set of life experiences fit with the other anyway. I think that too much of what is published today in literary magazines is merely a matter of lay-out and putting down what sells. Poetry is living. You know that, but I don't know how many others really understand. It doesn't really matter. You do what you can with the words when they come while you're riding the cattle car. They never last very long, but sometimes I think they'll help me and a few friends get through life in better shape than we might otherwise.

§

Whispers of Wrath

Last night
a plastic our son
inside a bird enamored with deadly colored liquids
whispered peace dreams to our ears
and glided across the ever waiting seas to feed on unarmed
women.
It landed on sleepy birds crushing their children's dreams.

Our heads disorganized,
we rolled over to other right side and stared eternally at the
lifeless ceiling
wondering when he'd return from Baghdad.

- Emmanuel Giambi

Bon Voyage

The poet packs
a suitcase that once
belonged to her grandmother.
Tattered and torn,
a deep red brown color
now known as the shade luggage
in Lands End catalogs.
It holds a few chapbooks,
a toothbrush, a tube of red lipstick,
several old movie stubs, 2 sweaters,
4 t-shirts, a pair of jeans and
a worn pair of pajama bottoms.
As she snaps the buckles closed
each one echoes
once twice...
go ahead and doubt something
doubt it once, twice,
but if you doubt it a third time
realize that it may not
have been true from the start.
Always hold that which
you hold dear.

-Sue Red

Gesture

I'd gone to see the ancient sites
Of Christians, Moslems, Israelites
when a Palestinian woman rose
to spit at my American clothes.
I'd already felt a guilty pain
for my new suit since we deplaned,
but her spoiling of my spun silk
helped absolve me of guilt.

- Diana Der-Hovanessian

Camels

On the desert,
that's next to the ocean,
camels lay like broaches.

At sundown,
they cried and
walked to Jerusalem.

The holy of Israel,
The holy of Islam,
The holy of Jesus,
A holy triumvirate of holies.

We must always remember
that even the camels
cried for peace.

- Barbara Bialick

PANAMA TEN

Two political prisoners were sitting
In their jeep with two
Panamanian National Guardsmen
Outside a bar in town

The two Panamanian Nationals
Went inside to check the bar
Leaving the two men
Handcuffed outside alone

Once inside the guardsmen spoke
To the bartender
In a language
I couldn't understand
When suddenly there was an explosion
Coming from outside the bar
And without looking the
Two guardsmen laughed
And downed their tequila and beers
While outside you could see the
Flames engulf the jeep
The two prisoners lit up
Like two scarecrows
Tossed into
A bonfire

- A.D.Winans

pushpa' poem

A Decrepit Map
Callused skin on my body
Ruptured by the cruel nature
Like a deserted and dry riverbed
In a summer
Is the native soil, my Rolpa and Rukum
My mutilated soil
Maimed by landmines
This callus on my soil
Cannot be cut away by surgery
And then be tossed away,
Like lifeless hairs
Stuck on the porcelain sinkhole rim.
Ghostly lizard crawls
On the dusty mirror
Hanging in the dirty wall
Of a dilapidated room
Where only emptiness
Catapults the carnal beauty
Of the mute image
Hidden under the layers of dust
Reveal my wounded Rolpa and Rukum
Like a decrepit map
Ripped by too many folds
Scratched and perforated by the worms.
The awful pain has butterflies
In my eyes
Of sullen
And morose sky.
(Rolpa and Rukum, the two remote districts in Far Western
Nepal, affected by the Maoist's People War)

- Pushpa Ratna Tuladhar

His Dresden Boots

Troubled below air force relics,
grandfather's flying boots buckled
with a certain red weight. They'd long lost
their tan and absorbed an umber wrinkle,

a day burnt from its morning peace.
I remember the embers in his eyes as he said
they were both on the floor and on his feet forever,
that he would never wear nor remove them again.
And that they talked to him. While he confessed,

heat flushed his scored face
like the leather's oiled-in penance,
like wood stained of pierced palms.
Like being judged.

I know what he meant now, how a man
carries his steps like stones to the grave.
How ears hear from far away - sounds
they know were there. How aftermath,
the silence and stillness, stay with you,
just like souvenirs.

(first appeared in The DMQ Review)

- Patrick Carrington

Colorless State of Existence

By Coleen T. Houlihan

I chose a rich scarlet shade,
the kind one does not wear everyday,
then carefully blotted.

Paper thin, with a weight,
not even detectable by ounces...
Once I laid a tissue across my palm,
blown my wind over transparent vessel's breast
and watched it rise,
take flight and land softly
at my feet.

In the car I lay it folded
in four across my lap
and allow it time to know me.
I talk to it like a soldier,
tell it this mission
is not a suicide or a slight against
the green grass which lays waving
along this highway road.

Another mile to go.

The Klan have always been
all over this land,
they knew my granddaddy when
he was too small to know
and they knew him after
he had grown too old to remember
a colorful state
of existence.

Several times I have seen them
from a distance,
white pointed hats devoid of nuances,
like a rainbow crafted
using White #5 or an uninhabited island
that screams "I am the world!"

The sign comes into view.
Underneath the smudge of mud
(the irked travelers form of dew),
I see the simple black print,
elegant letters stating
that I have arrived and
"This stretch of land
is cleaned by the Klu Klux Klan."

My window is unrolling.
The Kleenex unfolding.
My arm upholding
this sacred decree.

May the gash of red lips
flow from this tissue paper's kiss
and remind him there are colors
that describe the blood,
the rivulet of feelings which come from
up above and out through the human
capacity to feel,
and in through the human
desire to be valued for more than
body, money, skin-
recognized for soul and the ability to know
we all need understanding.

I let it go
and think,
May we be joined by these desires.

And with a little luck he will pick it up
and hold it slightly longer
than one should
a crumpled up tissue.

§

Accusation

I am torn by the present
I   as if i could paint it,
I   as if i could change it,
with my own mind. I can not.
This moment is being unwrapped by her death
when i am dreaming.
Unexpected past ghosts arrive
and she, my mother's voice
sentenced them,
perpetuated them.
Dancing shadows revive
the hidden burdens of yesterdays,
now   yearning calls every moment,
forgiving known faces, names and dates.
I allow them to wither
and become ashes of iridescent nuggets.
The church bell stops
her chants keep coming . . . .

- Beatriz Alba del Rio

The last view of mortal man
(For Don O'Brien)

Wishing for end to come, swiftly
But it lingers, lingers for 2 years … more
Abandonment of the spirit, please

But the soul lingers against the will
Give up, give up, give it all up
Perversity of nature, fight on and on and …

I sit, next to him, watching football
As we have for years and years and …
"What a bad call," I cry

I see a smile, I think
But he is "unresponsive"
His children, unresponsive, his wife dead

We sit alone now, just the two of us
Friends unwilling to see a dying man
He unwilling to be seen dying

What he had is gone, mostly
What he has left are memories
Recorded in a book, his only possession

"Port to port," The story of a young mans journey
into manhood
"Port to port," The story of a warship clearing for action
"Port to port," The memory of those who returned

For years we were "best buddies"
Tied by the sea, the sea, the sea
He the old chief, I the collector of stories

He sank a camel in the Suez Canal
The United States Navy paused briefly
On they're way to save the world in Korea, Indo-China

At the helm of the great ship
In the face of a typhoon
Even the admiral was sick

Military paradise: a .45 on your belt,
A 16-inch gun at your back
And an angry Turkish soldier with bayonet, fixed, at your
side

First class, Chief, Master Chief Petty Officer,
Principal character in this poem
You rise through the ranks as you fail

I stare out the window
As he has these many days
Fixed prison of his last view as a mortal man

We shared a beer at thanksgiving
We shared a beer, I drank it, at Christmas
I drank to his health on New Years

"I'm sorry, he's not here now,"
they said without emotion,
"Call the family."

"We buried him on Tuesday," she said
"Was there a service," I asked?
"No," she said and hung up.

- Steve Glines

A Cambridge Autumn Duo

i. Fort Washington

There's a plot some blocks from 10-250
down sidewalks crowded with granite
seats and sculpted beds of bloom,
where jargon of genome,
computational elegance and axiom
subside and, eating slots of sheet cake,
they float intuition on the grassy wind
streaming under language to roost
in fractaled fields of mind.

Not a place for hauling love
of country to attention – a gibbous moon
tops the dorms @MIT,
sentinels on the river, buoyed
by Spanish Japanese laughter,
by all manner of mental races,
a mutation of thrushes –
Spin instead perfumed ideograms,
codes drawn within, patterns piled out.

The flag's too big, too red
and blue, a predator in the park,
--a glorious dog-squat however you mow it--
people appear but just to pass
and gauge its iron rails against
the empty lots on either side,
odd frame for streets of science.

ii. Sunset on Charles River

Here comes a running fool
riding the day to its doom,
plucking pieces from the great puzzle –
from the space between branches,
from sun spark on water –
in the flash of a face glimpsed here
last December, while steering into the skid
when this road was a river of ice.

In pixel-glow dusk and
all agape with November,
I cruise the tree-glittered strand,
nose the leaf-litter -- entre chien et loup,
mapping the season of Kerberos.

We scribe lives beside the river,
hand over hand in concentric now.
You say, I'll show you
one hundred and one ways
I'll hold you always; who's to say
it's too much?

A school of sails ante-up
in the river basin,
rock to find center, masts
test gravity and good sense
with manacled jibes.
They tip sweet white bottoms
to the sky, madmen in formation --
there's nothing subtle about balance,
on or off -- it's just practice.

- Sarah Merrow

Four Poems after Xue Tao

By Jamie Parsley

1.

We will never share these flowers
that bloom this afternoon —
these lilacs that smell
like love would smell
if it could.

We will never share
the gut-deep sadness
we would feel when
the flowers fall
to the ground to fold
into themselves.

If you ever wondered
when I missed you most
simply think this —
I missed you when
the flowers bloomed up
to the sky and I missed you
when they shivered
and fell dying to the ground.

2.

Absently, I twist
grass stems and flowers
into the shape of
your heart
and mine—
entwining the one
to the other—
and send it to you,
the only one
who understand my poems.

It is almost noon and with it,
a sorrow like thawing earth
breaks the day apart.
The sparrows who fled
here in the fall
now sing songs so sad
I almost want to die.

3.

The wind—
like these flowers—
like this whole season—
is growing old and dying.

Does anyone know if—
or even when—
we'll see each other again?
If I can't tie your heart
to mine, why keep on tying
flowers into
heart-shaped knots?

4.

Do the lilacs—
growing fat on the branch—
know how overwhelming it is
when two people
who love each other
are not together?

When I look at myself
in the water, my tears
are the shapes of spoons.
Does the wind—
blowing this day
with such recklessness—
even know
what tears are?

§

Nuclear Fishin'

Observe nuclei undergoing fission—
A multi-dimensional
Potential-energy surface
Guiding the nuclear shape evolution—
From the ground state,
Through intermediate saddle points
To the configurations
Of separated fragments of fission.
Calculate and analyze five-dimensional
Potential-energy landscapes
Based on a grid of 2,610,885 deformation
Points, and find that observed fission
Features—the distributions of fission-
Fragment mass and kinetic energy
And the different energy
Thresholds for symmetric
And asymmetric fission—
Are very closely related
To topological features
In the calculated five-dimensional
Energy landscapes.

- George Held

Veterans of the Boy Scout War

By Gary Beck

I was so impatient that I kept waking up to see if it was Saturday morning yet. Tommy and Phip were supposed to call for me at five a.m. Even my camping gear looked restless. Besides, I was having a dream about bald men in long black coats that were chasing me. I kept tripping as they got closer, while windows were opening and people were throwing things at me like rattles, marbles and kazoos. I'd wake up, then each time that I went back to sleep the dream started again and the men got closer. They grabbed me. I started to fight and heard Tommy's voice saying: "Jeez. Ya dope. Wake up," and woke up to see Tommy pulling off my blanket and Phip climbing through the window.

Tommy was my best friend. We grew up together in Brooklyn on a working class street of connected brick houses. Tommy was the best baseball player in school and the leader in our adventures, with a talent for getting us in and out of trouble. I mostly went along with him, except if I thought something was really bad. I was becoming an avid, though secret reader, just beginning to think about what was right and wrong. Phip, however, was another country. He had always been dumb, but now he was getting weirder and weirder. I didn't want him hanging around with us anymore, but Tommy liked having a loyal follower and I didn't want to lose Tommy as a friend.

It was a few minutes after five and the first hint of light was licking at the chill spring air that smelled like ice cubes. I put on dungarees, a red and black checkerboard flannel shirt, thick sweat socks, boots and a denim jacket. Then I started to fix my backpack. Tommy silently helped me put on everything. My sleeping bag, pack, webbed belt with two canteens, ax, sheath knife and compass gave me a competent, military look. When we left we looked like well-equipped rebels going off to the hills to dynamite trains.

We took the IRT subway to the George Washington Bridge and the early Saturday morning passengers looked at our equipment, our Australian bush hats and us with drowsy curiosity and I-remember-when-I-was-young smiles. We had been going camping since we were twelve years old and had developed real woodcraft skills in the last two years. So we sat there like old pros, real cool, waiting for action.

By the time we reached the bridge it was a beautiful morning. We walked across the glimmering span that straddled the Hudson River like a many-tendrilled insect feeding on decay. We marched past the state line marker in the middle of the bridge and entered New Jersey like an invading army.

We stopped for a moment, leaning over the railing, looking way down at a service road that spiraled round and round until it reached the bridge. I took an apple from my pack and bit into it, juice rushing down my throat like the end of a drought.

"Hey. I got me a bomb. Look at me. I'm a B29," yelled Phip, snatching my apple.

"Gimme my apple, Phip," I demanded.

"Wadda ya mean, apple? This is a bomb. Cantcha see it's a bomb?"

"Will ya give me my apple?"

"Bomb bay doors open.... Bombs awayeee...."

He dropped it and we saw the red sphere plunge to earth. It

hit a car with a loud bang and we looked at each other in disbelief.

"Holy shit," yelled Tommy. "You hit that taxi, you asshole. Look at it. Look at that hole in the roof."

Far below us, the brakes screeched as the taxi stopped. The driver jumped out, looked at the roof, looked up and saw us hanging dangerously over the railing and started waving angry fists at us. He looked so funny that we started laughing harder and harder, until tears swam in our eyes and saliva sprayed from our mouths. We slumped down on the ground, rolling around and laughing hysterically. Phip kept yelling: "Bombs away," over and over.

"Hey, Tommy," I asked. "What if someone was in the back seat?"

We got up, rushed to the rail and looked down. The angry midget was still waving furious fists, but we could see that he was alone.

"Jeez," said Phip. "I'm gonna join the air force an' be a bombardier." This started us laughing like crazy again. Tommy calmed us down by saying: "Awright, you guys. He's gonna be after us, so let's get outta here."

We quickly picked up our gear and trotted towards the end of the bridge.

"Hey. Tommy," I whispered.

"Yeah?"

"That Phip's a real nut, ain't he?"

"You're not kiddin'. We better go a little faster, though I don't think that taxi can get up here before we reach the bus."

Tommy had been watching the taxi, which had started up the road leading to the bridge. We trotted a little faster, breathing hard, but still giggling when we thought of the apple.

We got to the bus stop without seeing the taxi and got on a bus that went north through Fort Lee. When the bus passed the town limits we got off and headed into the woods. Once we were out of sight of the road, we unrolled our sleeping bags, took out and loaded our BB guns, then moved out silently in single file, rifles in safety position, Indian scout fashion. We knew that the ominous forest silence, pierced by bird cries, forest sounds and crackling, rustling, swaying underbrush held brooding enemies contemplating our scalps, so we walked tense and alert, ready for an ambush.

Suddenly, a deep, gruff voice from nowhere asked:

"Where are you taking those BB guns, boys?"

We almost jumped out of our skins and whirled around. A big man with red jowls, and a bulging belly barely held in by a tan uniform, came out of the bushes. He had a shiny, round badge on his shirt, a huge revolver on his right hip and high, glossy black boots.

"Into the woods, sir," I piped up nervously.

"Are you boys sixteen?"

"No, sir. Fourteen," I said, which drew a disgusted look from Tommy, because he knew you had to be sixteen to legally use a BB gun. And Phip just stood there, slowly pushing his tongue between his lips, gazing gunfights at the big, black revolver.

"Well. Did you boys know that you can't have BB guns in New Jersey if you're not sixteen?"

"No, sir," Tommy and I answered, while Phip just stood there, wishing that he could outdraw and gun down the lawman.

"Well. You boys can leave them with me, in my office and pick them up on your way home."

"But we won't be going home until after midnight," Tommy cleverly said.

"Hmmm. I tell you what, boys. You can wrap your guns in a cloth and bury them here and dig them up on your way home. Would you be able to find them again?"

"Oh yes, sir," Tommy and I chorused.

His big hands waited patiently as Phip dug a shallow hole. Then Tommy carefully wrapped the guns, covered them with dirt and marked the spot with some sticks.

"Okay, boys. Have fun and don't get into any trouble."

"We won't, sir. So long," I said, as he turned and walked away.

"So long, boys."

We headed into the woods again. Tommy was savagely quiet, Phip was staring flaming pistols and I was relieved that the sheriff didn't lock us up for throwing the apple through the taxicab roof. After walking for about ten minutes I noticed we were circling back the way we had come, and that Tommy was making less and less noise.

"Hey, Tommy. Where we going?" I asked.

"Back to get the guns, dummy."

"That's it, Tommy," Phip chortled. "I knew you'd think of somethin'."

"Keep it down, Phip. I don't wanna announce we're coming."

When we got close to the disarmament conference site, we left our gear and approached the clearing stealthily. The birds were talking to each other and only stopping as we got closer, so we knew that the sheriff was gone. Tommy and I were lookouts, one on each side of the clearing, while Phip dug up the guns. Armed once more, we headed into the woods in single file, Indian scout fashion, ready for war parties.

We followed a tiny path that ran next to a stream. After four or five miles it seemed as if we were the only travelers who dared the hostile ambushes of the brooding forest.

"Awright, Billy. Start lookin' for a clearin' where we can pitch camp. And keep your eye on Phip."

"Where ya goin'?"

"I just wanna be sure that cop's not followin' us. Make a blaze with your ax every fifty yards or so and when I get near I'll hoot like an owl."

"Okay. See ya later."

"Hey. Phip."

"Yeah, Tommy?"

"You go with Billy and help find a campsite."

"Where ya going?"

"I'm just makin' sure that cop's not followin' us. I'll see ya in a little while."

"Oh. Lemme go with ya. We can dig a trap and when he falls in we can make him give us his gun to get him out."

"Ya know, Phip, sometimes you're real stupid. Go with Billy."

"Awright. But I think it's a great way to get a gun."

"You would. I'll see ya later."

Tommy left and I started walking again, leaving trail marks every fifty yards or so. Phip rambled behind me, shooting his BB gun at anything that moved. Birds, squirrels, rabbits, large insects, even rustling leaves, innocently going about their business, were suddenly deluged by grape-shot, ripping and tearing through the trees, humming like maniacal bees. Phip, jacking the lever of his gun, looked like a four-armed epileptic madman, shooting it out with shadows. He really was a jerk.

We walked a few more miles and found a good clearing for a campsite. I sent Phip to get kindling and firewood for the next two days. He changed from heavy walking boots to sneakers, because Tommy believed that nobody, not even Indians, could run fast in moccasins, let alone in boots. Gun in one hand, ax in the other, Phip stalked into the woods, intent on pillage. I started setting up camp.

First I set the tent fronting the stream. Then I dug a small moat around the tent, with a run-off drain to the stream, so that if it rained we would survive the flood. Next I dug a latrine about twenty-five yards from the tents and marked it with stakes and rope, so we wouldn't find it suddenly in the dark. Then I dug a garbage pit and a fire pit. I searched along the side of the stream until I found enough flat rocks to line the fire-pit.

I finished what could now be an oven or fryer and turned to my last chore, a lean-to for the supplies and firewood. I cut big branches with my ax and made the frame, then I covered it with medium-sized twigs and tied them together with grass. The lean-to would keep our supplies dry and it looked better than the pictures in the Boy Scout handbooks.

Phip had been industriously lugging in wood and had made a big pile that he stacked near the lean-to. And then I realized that Tommy hadn't come back yet.

"I wonder what happened to Tommy?" I asked. "He's been gone a long time."

"I dunno. Maybe he met a girl."

"Jesus, Phip. In the middle of the woods?"

"Wouldn't it be a great place to meet a girl? Nobody around for miles. We could take off her blouse and feel her knockers, an' maybe even let her have the old finger."

"You're crazy, Phip. If you had half a brain you'd be danger-ous."

"Oh yeah?"

"Yeah."

"Ya better watch watcha sayin', Billy, or we're gonna hafta have it out."

"Oh shut up, or I'll crack your head and let the sawdust out."

Tommy's irritated voice snapped us out of our confronta-tion. "Is that all you guys can do when I'm not around, get ready to fight? You didn't even hear my signal."

Tommy had come up on us stealthily and I was annoyed at myself for being caught twice in one day. Phip was real happy, wagging his tail and asking questions.

"Where ya been, Tommy?"

"To see the Queen of England, ya jerk. Where do you think I've been?"

"I don't know. What were you doin' all that time?"

"I wanted to make sure that nobody followed us. Then I followed two Boy Scouts until they camped about a mile away from here. Maybe we'll have some fun with them tonight."

"Yeah, Tommy? What kinda fun? Whatta we gonna do with them? Tell me. Tell me."

"Take it easy, Phip, I'll tell you later. Let's have somethin' to eat first. I'm starving. Hey. You guys did a real neat job here."

"Phip just brought the firewood. I did everything else. Doesn't it look great?"

"Yeah, Tommy, it does. But look at all the logs I got and they're real good ones too."

"Ya did a good job, Phip. Come on, let's eat. I'll cook and we can talk about a raid."

We hadn't eaten breakfast that morning and the tantalizing odors of frying bacon and eggs, sizzling in butter, poured out overwhelming messages to our stomachs. And when the coffee began to boil, the smells mixing in the cool, clear forest air made us mad with hunger. We ate like ravenous wolves. After the third cup of coffee, with cigarettes lit, we sat back full of food and power like ancient generals and began to plan the war against the boy scouts.

General Tommy O'Corman, with pointer in hand for use on the terrain map, began to develop the campaign that would defeat the unsuspecting foe.

"Now they're camped about a mile away. There's a thick clump of trees on one side, swamp and muck on another and an open area in front of a stream. This is what we do. Phip, you come through the trees from one side, covered with leaves and branches and carryin' the red lantern. You'll moan and screech and shake the bushes. Billy, you'll come in from the other side, climb into a big tree near them with your BB gun, caw like a crow and keep shootin' at them. I'll go in first, wrapped in a ground cloth, an' stay in front of the swamp ta make sure they don't run in an' get hurt or somethin'. I'll roar and growl like a bear."

"We could scare them to death," I said. "What if we just make some animal noises and leave it at that?"

"Why can't we let em run inta the swamp?" Phip asked. "Maybe they'll fall inta quicksand an' we can watch'em get swallowed up and sucked under, like in the movies."

"Ya know, Phip. You're real sick," I said in disgust.

"I'm warnin' ya, Billy boy, watch whatcha sayin' ta me."

"Both of you shuddup," Tommy ordered. "Well that's my plan. You guys got anything better?"

"I guess not," I muttered.

"No. No," Phip replied. "When da we start? When do we do it? Huh? Huh?"

"We'll leave here about nine o'clock, so when we get there the moon'll be up," Tommy explained. "We oughta catch them when they're relaxed and not expecting anything but a good night's sleep."

"Can we beat 'em up afta we scare 'em?"

"No, Phip. We don't want to hurt them. Let's just make 'em think they're bein' chased by bears an' spooks, an' stuff like that."

"I can't wait. Oh, Jesus. I can't wait."

And scooping up his ax, Phip began spinning around like a hopped-up dervish, throwing his ax into the ground and pulling it out again, yelling nonsense words in a mad chant:

"Horse blood....Ohhhh. Big gomps....Aya. Umba....Ohhh, Porp....Cut 'em. Cut 'em."

"Jeez, Tommy. He gives me the creeps sometimes. He's out of his head and getting worse."

"Aw. He's all right. Ya just gotta humor him. That's all."

"Not me. From now on that nut-job is not gonna go off his rocker when I'm around. I don't want to go camping with him again."

"Take it easy, Billy. You know we've all been friends for a long time. Let's just relax and have a good time together now that we're here."

"He's making it harder and harder to have fun anymore."

Finally Phip stopped raving and we spread our sleeping bags on the ground and sprawled in front of the tents, lazing in the hot sun. We lay there smoking and talking, mostly about girls and about how far the ones we knew would go. Phip couldn't get a girl to go near him, so he cursed a lot and told us what he'd do if he ever met a girl in the woods. Tommy told us about how he was making out with his girl friend Serena one day, when her father came home early from work.

"There I was on top of her, half undressed, an' she's sayin' do it, do it, I'm not scared. An' I was gettin' so hot that I was gonna do it, when all of a sudden I hear the door slam downstairs, an' her old man yells:' Anybody home?'

"I grabbed for my clothes an' shot inta the bathroom like a rocket an' hid behind the shower curtain. Her old man came up- stairs an' stopped ta talk ta Serena and that saved my ass. I got dressed while they was still talking and waited for my chance to get out of there. The next thing ya know the bathroom door opens and her old man comes in, drops his drawers, sits down on the bowl an' starts blowin' off farts like a mad whale."

Phip and I howled with laughter, picturing Tommy hiding in the shower and Serena's father, a tall, skinny plumber, sitting on the toilet, farting like wild.

"So what happened?" I demanded.

"Yeah, yeah. What happened? Tell us."

"I waited until he finished stinking up the joint an' went into his bedroom. Then I snuck downstairs real quiet an' went out the door."

"What would ya have done if he caught you in the bath- room?" I asked.

"Man, I woulda said I was local fart checker an' took off like a hot-assed cat. I almost cracked up when I heard him soundin' off like that an' I almost choked to death to keep from makin' any noise. He'd 've broken my head if he caught me there."

We laughed again and when we settled down I told them about the girl I was fooling around with. But even though I lied and made it seem like something was happening between us, after Tommy's close call it didn't go over too well.

A little later we went for a walk and wandered through the woods exploring old trails, looking for animal tracks and having target practice with our BB guns. I found an old rusty ax head, Tommy found an empty beehive that had some old honey combs and Phip fell into the stream.

We walked for three or four hours, just prowling through the woods, investigating anything that interested us, feeling that if we just walked a little further we would find something wonderful. But we didn't discover a lost civilization and started back to camp.

We were getting hungry again, so when we got back we made dinner, ate, cleaned the cooking gear, then just loafed around the campsite. Time passed, while the golden sun burned blood red and slowly set behind the trees. The sky changed from blue, to purple, to black and the stars appeared, making gleaming speckles on the night roof. Venus and Jupiter were blazing bright and whispered together, surrounded by lesser lights.

The moon rose, huge, dazzlingly bright, close enough to see seas and craters. We were silent for long stretches of time, just dark outlines, tipped with tiny burning coals from cigarettes. Tommy mentioned an old fight and Phip eagerly chimed in.

"Remember when we went down to Marine Park and got inta that fight?"

"Yeah. Yeah," Tommy answered.

But before they could get going about fighting I changed the subject. "Hey! Tommy. Remember the first hike we ever went on?"

"Yeah. I'll never forget that one. That was when we got lost before we ever left Brooklyn and it rained all day and all our food got ruined. We didn't eat anything until we got back to Fort Lee and had to swipe hot dogs from a stand, 'cause we only had carfare money."

"That was the time you threw your ax at Phip, remember?"

"Yeah, when he pretended to be a bear. I almost made him into a rug."

"That was a real funny hike."

"Oh it was real funny alright," Tommy teased. "I guess ya forgot how wet, cold an' hungry you were."

Time passed slowly, but we lay there contentedly, though we were starting to get impatient waiting for nine o'clock, thinking about how we would scare the boy scouts.

"Awright, you guys," Tommy announced. "I think we should start getting ready."

We put on our sneakers, Phip collected his branches and red lantern, Tommy took his ground cloth and I took my BB gun, then we filed into the woods. Silent and dangerous, we moved through the forest, making less and less noise the closer we got to their camp. When we reached the clump of trees in front of their camp we stopped for a last check of what each of us was going to do. The general staff was always thorough.

"Awright, guys. Now remember. I go first. Give me five minutes to get into position. Billy. You come next and pick a good tree, an' wait until you hear me growling before you start your attack. Phip. You wait here until you hear both of us, then move towards them slowly. But remember, go real slow an' wave the lantern and moan an' screech a lot. I'll hoot twice like an owl when its time to stop an' we'll meet back here. Don't make any noise comin' back an' don't get lost. Okay?"

Even though I had misgivings, I agreed. Phip was urgent to start.

"Yeah, yeah, yeah. Let's get going. Let's do it."

Tommy melted into the darkness and was gone. We waited tense and eager for the minutes to pass and listened to the night sounds of the forest, wondering which, if any, were Tommy.

"I'm going, Phip. Give me enough time to get into a tree. Okay?"

"Yeah, yeah. Shove off."

I slid into the dark, eerie shadows, twitching nervously at the sounds around me. I worked my way stealthily through the trees until I reached the edge of their camp. I found a big tree with a good branch and quietly climbed up and got into position.

The night was becoming hazy and clouding over, but it was still bright enough to see clearly. The Boy Scouts had built a huge fire which lit up the whole campsite, but it was so bright that they couldn't see into the woods. It was a sloppy camp, with expensive gear spread all over the place in a real mess. They were lying near the fire talking, and I could hear the sound of their conversation without understanding their words. It was hard to sit still in the tree and not laugh, thinking of the ghosts and bears lurking in ambush all around them, but I held it in and waited.

"Errarrh...."

"What's that, Donny?" the smaller boy asked.

"I don't know, but I'm scared."

"Errarrh...."

"Caw, caw...."

"There's something out there, Donny."

"Grrarr....Grrarr...."

"Donny, it's a bear. It's a bear."

"I'm scared. I'm scared."

"Caw, caw, caw...."

"Errarrh....Grrarrr...."

"Donny, it's not just a bear. There's something else out there."

"Ow, ow.... Something stung me."

"Ow.... It stung me too."

"What're we going to do, Donny?"

"Mooooan....Oooohhh....Oouh...."

"Donny. Look, look. It's a ghost, a red ghost. We gotta get out of here."

"Momma. Momma."

"Grrarr...."

"Caw....Caw...."

"Ooooh....Oooooh...."

"This way, Donny, they're all around us. We gotta run. Through the stream, quick. Follow me and stay close."

"Don't let them get me, Arnie. Don't leave me here. Momma. I want my Momma."

"Come on, Donny, or they'll get us. Hurry. Run. Run."

They raced through the clearing, splashed through the stream into the woods on the other side, frantically fleeing for their lives. The woods echoed with our laughter that sounded almost as horrible as our growling, cawing and moaning. I laughed so hard that I lost my balance and fell out of the tree. I landed on my back and just lay there, laughing and laughing. I finally got up and started towards the meeting place, still laughing. I could still hear the Boy Scouts crashing through the woods in blind flight, with Donny still calling for his momma.

As we got near the meeting place we announced our arrival with growls, caws and moans, in between gasping with laughter. We fell down in a limp pile, punching and pulling at each other, yelling all sorts of crazy things at each other.

"Holy shit, Tommy," Phip said, "Did you hear him crying for his momma?"

"I guess she don't love him no more, 'cause she sure didn't help him any. What do you say, Billy?"

"Man, I never saw anybody run so fast in all my life."

We repeated our animal noises and quoted the fleeing Boy Scout's last words and laughed and laughed until our eyes blurred and our stomachs hurt. We slowly headed back to camp, stopping often to lean against a tree and giggle, or suddenly slump down on the dark forest path and mimic the Boy Scout who cried for his momma. We reached camp and got right into our sleeping bags, too tired to do anything more than build up the fire. We went to sleep a gloating, victorious army, exhausted from night combat.

Sunday dawned a blazing sphere of calmness. The hot sun made us drowsy and last night's adventure kept us smug and lazy all day long. We just lay around and ate, smoked and talked about how we scared the Boy Scouts. We bragged about how well we imitated crows, bears and spooks. The day passed quickly and late in the afternoon we cleaned up the campsite, burned the paper garbage, buried the rest, packed our gear and headed into the woods, like weary soldiers remembering old battles.

Nothing much happened during our trek through New Jersey and when we got on the subway in Manhattan we dozed until we reached our station. We got off and said so long and I got home just after dark.

My folks asked me if I had a good time and wanted me to tell them what we did.

But all I said was: "It was okay," and went to bed early.

§

The house at 17 Emile Dunois

By Steve Glines

It was unusually cold for an August evening. The rain was unremitting and I ran the last thirty yards to the restaurant entrance. Once inside I saw him, back to the door, hunched over slightly in a French trench coat. Oddly I remembered the shape of the back of his head, his ears I guess. What a strange thing to remember after 30 years but it was unmistakably the back of the head of Dr. Roger Malina. Grey had replaced the jet-black hair of youth, but the back of his head, was unmistakable.

The last time I saw Roger was in 1972. He had just graduated from MIT and was heading to Berkeley, driving cross-country, for graduate school. In these pre-Internet dark ages I lost track of him but occasionally would hear about how he had done this, had done that, had done very well or so the gossip many times removed had said.

I met Roger by accident. In 1970 I arrived in Cambridge Massachusetts with all my worldly belongings strapped to the back of my Yamaha motorcycle. I had intended to go to MIT but I couldn't afford it. I had intended to share an apartment with a high school friend but when I arrived in Cambridge he had moved into a smelly, overcrowded Fraternity house filled with mock sophistication and demonic seniors. The Frat boys took me in telling me I could pledge when I got the cash together to attend the 'tute. A few months later some of the ex-frat members rented an apartment and asked me to join them. Roger was one of them.

When the Internet made it easier to reconnect lost souls I found Roger at the University of California at Berkeley. Somewhere along the line he mentioned that he was thinking of turning his mothers house in Paris into a pancion. I told him to put me down as the first tenant. I can't remember how long ago that was, early 1990's I think. Getting to Paris and bringing my wife, who has never been to Europe, became as goal ... as soon as our children became self-sufficient. About 2 years ago I emailed Roger with our plans. Just after Christmas 2005 I emailed him our detailed itinerary. In April Roger emailed back that he would be in Boston in August to deliver his son to Tufts University.

I got a telephone call. It was Roger. In his lovely English accented voice he announced, "I'm here. Let me know where you'd like to meet." To an American Roger sounds English but to an Englishmen he sounds completely American. Roger was born and grew up in Paris, went to prep school in England, and spent most of the next 30 years in Cambridge Massachusetts, Berkeley California and Aix-en-Provence France. The accent I was hearing, have always heard when I think of Roger is a remnant of his grade school days in England.

When I saw his face it hadn't changed much save for the grey beard on what I remember to be a boyish clean-shaven undergraduate. Time has been kind to Roger. Our chatter picked up as if it had never stopped. My greatest fear was that we might not have anything to say after 30 years. Roger is an astronomer, a cosmologist, interested in what happened during and just after the big bang. He's helping to build a satellite called SNAP that will attempt to map any fine structure in the "Dark Matter," that esoteric stuff that most theories of physics predict make up 90% of the mass in the Universe. Heady thoughts and the kind of things I love to chat about and can with Roger. If there is granularity, a fine structure to Dark Matter, can it form a black hole? Could we tell the difference between a black hole made of Dark Matter and ordinary matter? What happens at the Schwarzschild radius? Can a black hole made of Dark Matter evaporate the same way an ordinary Black Hole can? Lets put Stephen Hawking on it so he can finally get the Nobel.

Nothing had changed except age but we did not have the luxury of endless chatter. We brought each other up to date the same way we would have if we had not seen each other for a month or two. I got married, had kids. He got married, had kids. The passing of time creates brevity of talk that none of us really like. Can the life of a man, great or not, be summed up in an hour's conversation? Yes, it sometimes has to be and can if you know the back-story.

As we finished dinner Roger handed me a small purse made of Provincial cloth, lined with silk and containing two brass skeleton keys. These were the keys to his pancion in Paris. We had never discussed the always-touchy subject of rent for the week and I was prepared to pay whatever he asked. Roger is one of those people I implicitly trust. But before I could broach the subject he said, just make a contribution to "Leonardo." "Leonardo" is the reason my trip to Paris is possible and the key to understanding who Roger is.

From Southern California to the suburbs of Paris

During World War Two the American military was interested in perfecting rockets for obvious reasons. Out in the desert of the American southwest there was a group of scientists and engineers interested in exploring space with rockets. It was an uneasy marriage. One of those looking upwards was Frank Malina, a rocket scientist, Rogers's father. He developed a small rocket called a WAC Corporal that could be flown alone or atop a German V2 with instrumentation designed to explore outer space. America's first space program was born. Frank went on to found the Jet Propulsion Laboratory at Caltech and the Aerojet-General Corporation, a manufacturer of rocket engines.

But that wasn't enough. Frank Malina walked away from a career building rockets, moved to Paris to become a kinetic sculptor, found a Salon and raised a family. Along the way Frank Malina founded the magazine "Leonardo." "Leonardo" is an academic journal devoted to the merger of arts and science.

Its manifesto states:

"Although visual or plastic fine art is one of the oldest fields of human endeavor, there are no journals of international origin that are by and for the artists themselves. There are numerous journals for aestheticians, for historians of art and for the general public. This situation, as regards the failure of artists to write on aspects of their own work, is partly due to the highly individual character of artistic expression, but also because a strong opinion has held sway that artists should leave verbal description and analysis of their works to other professions. When we look at the basic and applied sciences we find that workers in these fields, who are no more skilled than artists with the written word, are expected to write about original aspects of their work. These writings are of benefit to their colleagues, and help to expand and improve man's understanding of nature and to advance the use of this understanding for man's purposes."

The House at 17 Emile Dunois had been built to be the studio of Portuguese sculptor, Ernesto Canto da Maia in the first decades of the 20th century, during the "Modern Era." The history of this wonderful house can be read on the website of Leonardo-on-line:

Boulogne sur Seine also known as Boulogne-Billancourt, was, in the beginning of the XXth Century, a booming place. Industrial activity - the Renault factories, LTM telephone equipment, the cinema Studio Billancourt were installed in this socialist municipality. Innovative architectural and urbanistic experiments were being made by Perret, Tony Garnier, Mallet Stevens and Le Corbusier. Paul Marmottan gathered his collections there. Artists like Juan Gris, Vieira da Silva and Arpad Szcenes, the historian Salomon Reinach, the art dealer Henry Kahneweiler lived there and the tradition of opening their houses on Sundays, joining together writers, critics, the artistic vanguards was one that Frank Malina would recreate in the 1950's and 60's.

Several sculptors had installed there their ateliers, such as the Russian prince Toubetskoy, Joseph Berard, Landowski. Canto da Maia, Lipchitz, Imenitoff, Max Blondat were some of the younger artists who settled in Boulogne after the war. Canto da Maia lived in Boulogne from 1923, having bought sculptor Landowski's old atelier. Later he built no.17, where he never actually lived, as he separated from his wife Mathilde soon after construction was completed. He remained living in Boulogne until, participating with success in the Parisian artistic scene. In his work, the stylisation and elegance of decorative arts are used to express his particular kind of delicate, melancholic intimacy. Canto da Maia returned to Portugal in 1938. Matilde and his children remained in the no. 17 until it was sold to Marjorie and Frank in 1954.

Roger grew up in this milieu of artists, writers and, of course, scientists. I asked Roger if he had any inclination to be an artist himself. "No," he laughed, "I spend all my free time associating with artists." Frank Malina's legacy is a vision of the beauty to be found both in the heavens and crafted by the hand of man. It was the passion of Leonardo da Vinci himself. "Leonardo," the magazine, the organization, and the vision has become Rogers's passion. The Universe and the Artist; The Universe as artist; The Artist as creator of the Universe.

We wondered into the rainy night and into a melancholy mood. When you are young everything is possible. We are no longer young; everything is no longer possible. It's hard to look back. As we parted he drifted off into the night and into his own thoughts. I too drifted off into a swirl of memories I had forgotten and rewritten over the years. I prefer the rewrites, the myths, to the original. We all do.

§

Over life (about my dead aunt)

By Irene Koronas

I look through the closet for the appropriate black shirt and find one that needs to be altered, a textured cotton blouse. "If I open the side seams it will hang better, and let my protruding stomach look flatter. It'll look good with my long black skirt." Athena checks the mirror, while talking to herself, to see if she looks thinner this morning. But of course her shape is still round and her youth so far behind her that she forgets what it was, how all the men found her attractive. Her aunt once called her a slut in front of all her aunts' girls that worked for her. This embarrassment takes years to forgive, especially, since it was said with Athena's daughter right there. "Yes. That's right. I'm a slut. So what." Athena retorts with defiance dripping from the side of her mouth like a tiger ready to eat a recent kill.

In three days the funeral will take place at the Greek Church. Thee just wanted to be buried without any wake or fanfare. My cousin tells me she was okay yesterday morning after having a heart attack at the nursing home where she had been for a week after being in the hospital a week from over medicating herself. Imagine eighty seven years old and she was still trying to tell people what to do for her by ordering them here and there, get me this get me that. What an incredible old hawk she was. I called the priest to let him know and asked if he would be kind enough to visit Thee in the intensive care unit. An hour after he left she died.

This might sound strange, but when someone I know dies I usually hear from them one to three days later. We talk about what the dead person wants me to say to someone who is still alive. This morning I think, geeze, I haven't heard from Thea maybe she won't talk to me. As I'm driving to my local coffee haunt I hear a voice.

"Athena I'm afraid"

"I've been waiting for you"

"Where am I"

"I don't know Thea, follow the light, ask for forgiveness, talk to Jesus directly. Ask him to have mercy on you."

"I'm afraid"

My morning drink is now tea since the coffee is making my stomach upset along with some members of my family. It feels like I'm a mafia moll being mulled over by the Italian side of a construction crew. They are always trying to reconstruct my life. So here I am sipping my tea with young gorgeous intellectual people with laptops and cell phones. How conspicuous can I be with my short white hair dressed in mourning black and red sneakers. Yeah. I'd say I'm about as obvious as a six-foot turtle trying to write down what dead relatives tell me and it's so silly and movie like that I want to melt my pen and eat it.

"Thea everyone you know will be in the light." this doesn't sound true to me since most of her friends are hard core murders, gamblers, lie about everything from stolen merchandise to the change due her and she loves whores (not her niece being a whore but other girls) the whores who do what she asks them to do, like call and make threatening calls to the local bookmaker or a tenet who won't leave one of her apartments, the list continues into drug addicts etc. so, I think to myself how can you tell her to look for the light. Then it occurs to me her mother and father and all the Greek aunts and uncles are all good god fearing people and they will be there waiting if she can get herself together enough to float toward the light. Okay. I feel better about this.

"Who will take care of my son"

"He is old enough to care for himself," words escape from my mouth, "Jesus when will this all end. Do I have to still do your bidding? And do I have to invite him over on holidays when I don't even know how to cook?"

"What about his drug habit. Will you tell him it is not worth the numbing out? Will you tell him I see his father and that the body is dead but I feel young again."

"Maybe" I quip. This can't be happening. What the hell am I talking to?

"Why wouldn't you"?

"Because you're dead and we are having this conversation in a coffee shop and he'll think I've lost it."

"Ha ha ha" my aunt is cracking up over a situation I find ridiculous. She likes this. Me being here taking down what she is telling me. I must be nuts.

I hear her laugh as if we were together at the dog track with her body guard/do right gal/chauffer, Marge. Marge had a way of making us laugh about stupid stuff, like did we see how that dog took a piss before the race started, Marge points over toward the fence, don't ya see that means it'll win this race, ya gotta play it to win. "Here Marge put twenty to show." my aunt is still laughing as she hands Marge the money. Usually, it is my job to run to the windows to place bets and to pocket the ten she gives me to play. But, I prefer to take my money home so I can buy groceries for my three children. Even when my father took me to the horse track, I thought all the waiting around and throwing money on animals who ran around a track, stupid, just plain stupid, yet, thinking was not what I was being paid to do.

"Look let my son think about what your saying, give him time to think. You know he thinks your half crazy anyway, and he believes what you tell him, he knows you don't lie." my aunt is on a roll now. "I don't give a shit if he thinks your crazy. This is about his life, his children. We need to let them know there is a hell. We need to tell him to get himself off whatever he's on. Now do it. When you die there will be no one who is open to receive the messages of the dead. I'm sorry. I'm sorry I treated you the way I did, for calling you a slut and thinking you were stupid." I'm enjoying this confession. She needs to tell me she's sorry and it's about damn time.

"I know you have forgiven me but I also know the damage I have caused to my family, all in the name of fear. I'm still afraid. Let me continue confessing because the more I talk the lighter it becomes. Oh God don't let me stay here, have mercy on me and everyone who has been in my life. Is that you. Oh. I can see my mother my father, so close." Thea is fading off my radar screen.

This is enough to send me home to bed or to my computer so I can write more quickly what is happening while I listen to this stuff like it's real. Maybe, this is all just grief masking itself as a story. 'Whatever'. I'll just finish this and move on to the next 'whatever' in my life.

"There are no secrets," Thea interrupts me while I'm trying to get some housework done, "no four million dollars." the mystery of whose got the money is unraveling. "I know my son thinks we have millions, but, we don't. I spent it gambling on the damn scratch tickets. Hundreds of them a week, all the money went toward my habit of taking a coin and rubbing off the silver to get to numbers, numbers rigged to never match, this expense took his inheritance."

"Thea, how am I suppose to change a sixty year old man. You taught him how to live and now you're taught him how to die. What do you expect of me?"

"Athena you have to do this for him, understand?"

"Look, I can't change him. Why don't you visit him yourself and tell him what you are telling me."

"He isn't receptive to the dead, like you are."

"Hell. What does that mean? Try visiting him in his dreams."

"The drugs keep him from feeling or hearing anything."

"I've done enough for you to last me ten life times. Please don't ask me to do anymore."

"You think you're so smart. Don't you know you're already written this down. Sometimes it is so easy to sucker you in. "

"Yeah. Well I can drop this pen and call it quits."

"Not until you finish this, honey."

"Okay, what else, and forget me talking to him. Maybe after I revise this story I'll mail him a copy."

"That'll work. You're a sure bet Athena."

"Thanks"

"Thank you"

"Yeah yeah"

"Tell my son I'm sorry for not letting him go, for not trusting in love to help him to become a business partner."

Her son has been skimming off the top of the profits from the construction of apartment buildings and rentals, because, he says his mother won't give him what's due him.

"Thea where are you now, what's going on, are you there?"

She is not communicating with me anymore. This feels real good. Now I can get on with living. Free from dead talk. My dark clothes help to continue the process of letting go. Relatives have begun to arrive, the caterer selected, the house is clean. My cousin has set the ball on the wheel and we are prepared like dogs at the starting gate. This is becoming a very familiar ritual: incense, prayers, priest in long robe, limousines, crying, more black clothes, children with questions, fathers having a smoke outside, stories, stories, stories ready to try on. The short black jacket, the long black blouse, black pumps, brown boots, (do I dare wear brown), black necklace, thin gold earrings, grandmothers' gold bracelet. The death chant begins, the candles are lit and I will miss this matriarch, this leader of a gang of desperate women with little hope for a future beyond their poor neighborhood upbringing. The women who have remained loyal will be in the back of the church, deceased, drugged, smoke ridden, waiting to get the hell out into the fresh air, waiting to play the number of Thea's death 311 the number that will get them a better life, waiting to buy a scratch ticket every day from now on in memory of Thea with hope that she will kiss the card for luck.

The wheel stops

In black suits

We carry her body for the last time out of a church she hated being in and only spent maybe ten minutes in when someone she knew died. She also gave lots of money to the priest in hopes of buying her way into heaven. Her coffin is the best one made and her favorite flower, white carnations, drape over like so many poker chips.

"What time did you say it was?"

"One p.m."

"I think I'll play the number 1583"

"Is that you Thea?"

§

Veer-Zara and Bombay's Bollywood

By Molly Lynn Watt

With all the things gone wrong in the world, have you ever found yourself wishing to opt out for an evening to see "Singing in the Rain" or "Sound of Music" for the first time? A movie that bathes your soul in sweetness and light rather than giving you a kick in the gut? A movie, even if set against a backdrop of war or gang menace, that you might leave with the feeling people love each other, life is good with music to sweeten your outlook, brighten the very skies above and obscure politics, at least for a night.

My husband, Dan, and I felt that way. We sought a film to brighten our skies, therefore we rejected a fourth viewing of Satyajit Ray's moving and significant and sad film "Patha Panchali" showing — again — at the Harvard Archive. Likewise we rejected all the American movie listings. (We'd already seen "Shall We Dance?" – the marvelous Japanese original and the recent Richard Gere triumph.) We noticed a small ad — Bombay Cinema presents "Veer-Zara" at the Capital Theater in Arlington. We looked up the write-ups to see what it was about. The movie has thousands of uncritical references on the Internet, it has opened all over the world and is discussed on English, Hindi and Muslim websites, with comments written from as far a field as South Africa and Norway. It is a phenomenon. But after reading the story synopsis we dismissed it as a soap opera.

We stayed home and read the Sunday New York Times instead. As luck had it, the Times magazine focused on films. I read the film director Mira Nair's memoir on Chai, that deliciously spiced Indian tea, then turned to the fiction writer Suketu Mehta's first person piece, "Bollywood Confidential."

He wrote that people watch Bollywood movies because the

movies are "pre-cynical, Bollywood believes in motherhood, patriotism and true love." He claims westerners dismiss Bollywood as melodramatic, but asserts the movies are redeemed by including singing. "No blockbuster special effects, no interplanetary spaceships, no lone Americans single-handedly taking on armies of brown people — just singing, and respect to mothers." He further establishes that Bombay is a city with contrasts so extreme that only movies that make no claim to represent morality can do justice to it; a city where confronted by difficult moral choices — the loss of life or love — the protagonists burst into song. The recipe for Bollywood movies apparently includes between 4 and 15 songs. Where western moviemakers have almost abandoned musicals as films must compress onto home TV screens, Hindi films are shown mainly in large theaters where sweeping vistas carry off the larger than life dreams.

Dan went to the library and took out Suketa Mehta's book Maximum City – Bombay Lost and Found. I turned immediately to the chapter on "Distilleries of Pleasure" and learned that Bollywood filmmakers are all big dreamers who make mainstream movies of collective dreams for a billion people. Hindi film directors detest the term Bollywood. The Bombay industry is older than Hollywood because the American Industry started on the East Coast before moving to Hollywood, and the Lumiere Brothers brought cinematography to Bombay in 1896 a few months after it debuted in Paris.

The Indian entertainment industry is worth $3.5 billion – minor in relation to the global $300-billion entertainment industry. But it is the world's biggest movie industry when it comes to production and viewers: 1,000 feature films, 40,000 hours of TV programming, 5,000 music titles exported to seventy countries. Mehta says that "every day, 14-million Indians see a movie in one of 13,000 theaters; worldwide, a billion more people a year buy tickets to Indian movies than to Hollywood ones. Television is galloping in." The country has 60 million homes with TVs, 28 million with cables, homes getting a choice of 100 channels. (Bill Clinton, on a visit to India, is reported to have observed that Indians have more channel choices than Americans.) Hollywood movies make hardly a dent in India, making up barely 5% of the market in India. Indian movies are dubbed or subtitled in a dozen foreign languages — French, Mandarin, Malay and popular with Soviets, Israelis, Palestinians, Dominicans, Haitians, Iraqis, Iranians. And Indian people living abroad take their families to a show to maintain ties homeland ties and cultural values.

Dan and I have often talked of taking a trip to Bombay. Instead, we zipped out to the Capital Theater in Arlington to see Veer-Zara. No senior discount, the charge a universal ten bucks. We entered the Capitol's largest screening room already packed with 3 and 4 generation families in a hubbub of talk and picnic baskets. In scanning the crowd, we eventually noticed two white faces besides our own, but they, unlike us, were enmeshed in a larger mixed family group. When, at 8:30 PM, the curtain opened for this 3 hour and fifteen minute show — no ads, no shorts, no trailers — everyone clapped and cheered. We were excited, too, as when we were children and our family took a night out to the cinema — a major event. We were not to be disappointed.

The story, well, the story starts in a jail cell and quickly flashes back to a girl – Zara - and a boy –Veer — meeting by accident, she — stunningly beautiful, he —gorgeously handsome. Zara is crossing physical and as well as metaphoric borders taking her Bebe's ashes from Pakistan back to India, this, her last promise to her beloved Bebe – a person I take to be her ayah. This journey establishes the uncompromising virtues of bravery, independence and goodness embedded in her heart. The bus on which she travels topples off the edge of the road spilling passengers down the side of a ravine. All must be rescued. Zara is the last person rescued in a daring helicopter pick-up. It becomes immediately apparent she is a person deathly afraid of heights. Her rescuer is Veer, and the audience screams with delight as he dangles off the end of a rope to swoop her to safety. It is love, restrained and exuberant, at first sight, well, first clutch really as they sway in each other's arms against a truly sky-blue sky on a rope swinging from a hovering helicopter.

A couple of problems immediately become clear with cloudy complexity – Zara is already betrothed to a business client of her father's in an arranged marriage. She is Pakistani. She is Muslim. Veer, a Hindu, lives in a village in India. None of this bodes well for the restrained couple clearly trying not to be in love.

I won't give it all away, although the story is not even half of it. Suffice it to say — a young woman civil rights lawyer is key to its resolution. She believes in rightness, not riches, and her first case is this hopeless one of a man who has languished in prison for 22 years because he will not dishonor the woman he loves by explaining his innocence, well, really, by talking at all.

The scenes are lush and musical, streams of golden sun shine on fields of golden grasses, and meadows of marigolds, while mists rise from ponds to shroud the standing mountains in metaphors. You can taste the samosas, as you watch villagers pulse and dance with joy. Even the rainfalls, with bold allusions to "Singing in the Rain," are sensual, and you may find yourself yearning for a downpour to warm your heart. The story depends on a suspension of disbelief and we are delighted to oblige. It is a full-blown fairy tale of good values no longer in tact in the world, and the audience knows and loves the songs and the actors.

A back-story to this movie is that the director Yash Chopra used previously unused tunes by a premier composer for Bollywood, the late – by 30 years —Madan Mohan. And one of the actors, Lata Mangeshkar, 75 years old, sings nine of the songs to huge cheers by the packed audience. We join the clapping and cheering; we're smiling really broad grins.

At 11:45 as we stand outside at last waiting for a bus home. A woman in a sari stands beside me and asks, "have you seen any other Indian movies?" I tell her about the Sayajit Ray's Patha Panchali trilogy. She'd not heard of it. She rattled off a dozen must-see Bollywood movies I should rent on DVD. I'd not heard of them. She tells me she has been coming to the Capital Theater in Arlington for 30 years to see Indian films. I also have been coming to the Capital for as long, but never noticed Bollywood movies advertised before this one. She asks, "How do you understand the movie in Hindi?" I reply, "subtitles!" "Oh" she laughs; she hadn't noticed the subtitles. We both laugh. "Well," she says, "this was the most expensive movie ever made - $10-million." $10-million sounded reasonable to my jaded American notion of movie costs. And although I've researched on the Internet, I have not yet confirmed her figure.

The next night I wanted to go see Veer-Zara again, but that would have been excessive. Instead I've been dreaming the songs and the waving fields of grain and the pulsing dance and the beautiful stars and colorful clothing ever since. I wish I knew the words as I hum and smile out loud. I wish I owned the CD for the singing or the DVD for the whole experience, but our TV screen is too tiny to hold its exuberance.

§

Rocket Scientist

By Laurence McKinney

The snow was still spotting the ground around the muddy test site; the moist March sky hovered over us in dull gray clouds. There were few to witness the tense activity as we ran through the final pre-launch protocols.

"Battery reading?" "Positive!"

"Launch pad?" "Clear!"

"Wind speed?" "Zero!"

Fueled and fully loaded, the rocket gleamed in shiny metallic bronze, standing upright on three triangular aluminum fins. The nose was a little funky, but there's a limit to what I could do with a ball-peen hammer and body filler. After sanding and painting, it was fine from any side. We were going to show the Soviets what American ingenuity could accomplish. Sputnik had humbled us the year before, beep-beeping across the sky, thumbing its commie nose. It beat us to the punch. The final horror was the hurried launch of the sleek US built Vanguard.

It was all on television. The family sat in the living room, transfixed as we listened to the countdown, three, two, one, just like Commander Corey on Space Patrol. Now we were at the threshold of space, which we proceeded to trip right over in prime time. The motor ignited, there was a billowing cloud of white smoke and the silver bullet slowly rose from the pad, vibrating just a little bit. Then it rose less slowly. Then it sort of stayed put on its flame as if somebody at mission control had just had a second thought. Then it slowly sank back down to the pad. But it didn't stop, it got worse. It slowly toppled over on the side opposite the gantry and blew up, just blew up, in front of the entire world.

A week later WRGB was offering basic Russian in the morning, at 6:00 A.M. I decided to get to know my opponent. I wanted know what Ivan knew. The time slot was murder, however. One week later, I realized these people didn't even have a normal alphabet. N was an H and they had weird letters with names like "yackishnak", which actually sounds a little like "Caddyshack" but looks like a trapezoid. No wonder they got up there first, their children were geniuses just to learn how to write it. This six AM torture wasn't going to prepare me fast enough.

With the help of a Russian phrase book by father had purchased and the WRGB pronunciation drills, I had it worked out in a week. Soon I could say, in perfect Russian "Strasviche tovrish, Mir y dhrushba! Nakonyets ya svoboda!" "Welcome comrade, Peace and Friendship. At last we're free!" I could see Lt. Ivan calling for his general. "Here is the person to put in charge of Loudonville, General Kropotkin! I'd be the boy commissar. That would shut them up until I could figure out how to abuse their trust and blow up something.

However the Russians never invaded, so my clever ploy was a total waste of time for nearly forty years. Now exactly same phrase, will start a friendly conversation with any Russian émigré. The short life of secret agent Laurence, boy commissar, soon re-crystallized into Laurence, boy rocket scientist, and we were headed for the moon. Or at least over the McNamee's barn.

Model rocket clubs these days can't imagine what it was to make your own in 1958 from scratch. We couldn't buy a "rocket motor" to snap into a pre-built hobby rocket. Today super-techno geek rocket amateurs with huge real rockets launch once a year in the desert, the Burning Man of do-it-yourself Sky Captains, but in the fifties I was scanning the Scientific American cover to cover. One month, The Amateur Scientist section had plans for a four-foot tall solid fuel aluminum sounding rocket, including the fuel recipe, zinc dust and sulfur. Burns at the rate of five feet a second. Any laboratory supply house has both; they're perfectly legal. Still are.

Within days the heavy carton arrived. I had prepared static firing tests of the rocket motor in three directions. That is I mixed it up, funneled a half-cup of the greenish powder into a brass pipe hammered shut at one end, and stuck in a fuse and stuck the pipe in the lawn. Would the thrust send it to China? The next was anchored in a cement block at a 45-degree angle, and finally, on a sled with clamps anchored horizontally.

The first two demonstrated one problem. Five feet a second is much too fast for what anyone could consider a controlled burn. This creates a launch sequence expressed simply as "three, two, one, zero, Fah-TOOOM". The rocket shoots straight up on a pillar of white smoke. No stately Tom Corbett rise on a tail of flame, not even the standard bottle rocket hissing up on its arc of orange sparks. More like a July 4th fireworks mortar. One "Fah-TOOM" and it's over except to clean up the zinc oxide.

The first test Fah-TOOM'd a belch of white smoke but buried itself no further in the ground. The second Fah-TOOM'd at an angle like a carbide cannon, but much more smoke. The last test was the last test because it Fah-TOOMED right out of its clamps, shot off the sled and nearly embedded itself in the clapboard of the house. "What's all this?" called my father, standing in the doorway. He'd been awakened from an afternoon siesta in the Barcalounger. There was a chunk out of the front of the house and I moved in front of it.

"Don't worry, I'm wearing my goggles". He retreated back inside the house.

Inside I was shivering because the brass pipe that had carved out a piece of the house had missed me by less than six inches. Until the day they died, neither parent knew about that one. On one hand, it was a sure-fire rocket fuel. On the other hand, after the Sunday afternoon tests, we moved the launch pad to Danno McNamee's large driveway and gave it a subtle tilt towards his huge front yard.

Danno's mother inherited a small brokerage firm, Cooley & Company, and her entrepreneurial husband Dan had renamed it First Albany and was hoping his four sons would follow in his footsteps. Ultimately, Danno's younger brother George McNamee did just that, and now First Albany has offices all over the place like Merrill Lynch. That day, however, George was hiding behind the door as we unrolled the launch wires back to the garage.

It wasn't a sleek Vanguard, it was barely two feet tall. The rocket nozzle was actually fashioned from the bolts that held the fins on. It stood on a small platform in the middle of the driveway in the midst of mud and melting snow, waiting for the call to flight. We had a little switchbox and the firing mechanism was simplicity itself: a flash bulb with glass removed, making a little cup with a squib that could be fired with a battery. We had no idea what a Vanguard cost, but the originally christened ARSOL–1 (from the Amateur Rocket Society of Loudonville, until we took a look at the initials and changed the name) was a cheapie. Ten dollars would have been a high bid.

Trying to sound very official, we started the countdown. "Zero minus one minute and counting."

Mrs. McNamee quickly ducked behind the screen door.

After these long we had finally arrived at the mantra we had all been preparing for.

"Zero minus ten, nine, eight, six, six, five, four, three, two, one, launch ...." I threw the switch.

It stood for a moment. My veins turned to ice. This couldn't be happening, not a misfire. Then came a "pfffft" and a half-hearted cough sending it about fifty feet in the air, just high enough to curve over the barn before dropping heavily onto a flat side roof covered with oxidized red galvanized panels. The shock must have redistributed the fuel because now it tried to do the "Fah-TOOM" excepting that it was horizontal, more like a bazooka. What was it with these horizontal missiles from hell we kept launching?

Trailing white smoke, it shot across the McNamees back yard at a height of about twenty feet before dropping to the ice-patched lawn where, with a final burp, it pin-wheeled to a pit stop next to the porch where it lay smoking and steaming like a deranged plumbing fixture. We gazed at the scene in disbelief and disappointment, only lightened by the fact that George was seriously amazed at what his older brother was up to.

Mrs. McNamee was also seriously amazed at what she'd witnessed, imagining what might have happened to their pony, also downwind from the launch vehicle and the Loudonville cosmodrome was shut down forthwith before we even had a second chance. We calculated that it had actually gotten about twenty feet higher than the Vanguard, and at least fifty feet in the air is horizontally. The Soviets were spared again, and my interested shifted to Tesla coils.

§

Meeting at the Pass

"I know sometimes it isn't easy being my friend."
--Doc Holliday in Lawrence Kasdan's Wyatt Earp

By Afaa Michael Weaver

Apples look like hearts. There are googles of heart shaped Valentine's candies. Chocolate is so much sweeter in a heart's shape. I don't think I would ever want to touch a human heart. Like most people, I'm satisfied to know I have one but not really interested in seeing it or anyone else's. I saw a horror movie once when I was in the third grade. This evil spirit snatched a woman's heart right out of her body, held it for a moment and then put it into her own body. I couldn't sleep for two months. It's enough to know we have this slippery thing that we occasionally feel as it beats inside us, and we know we should be nice to it, but now and then we sneak things like french fries and potato chips. A few won't hurt this mystery that sends blood to a zillion places.

The Treehouse was the third floor of a Victorian house owned by the Butlers, lovely people who fell in love in the third grade at home in South Carolina and had been married for fifty years, both of them in their eighties, spry and loving. My own marriage had failed, and I retreated to this apartment, the back of which was held in the thrust of leaves from maples three stories tall and more. The house was in Philadelphia's University City neighborhood, in walking distance of several nice coffee shops, including one called Chimes. I bought a computer and buried myself in writing. I was determined to have no secrets and began writing about my relationships. But sometimes your secrets know you when you don't know them. The summer was otherwise dull, and the winter, lonely, cold, and full of new feelings that come when things fail.

One day that following spring Roger Allen Jones came walking down my block stepping like Sporting Beaseley in his sport jacket and too big sneakers. He was a poet like none other and knew me by my book Water Song. I was on my front steps, and as he came nearer he sang out my name in operatic style.

"Michael S. Weaver." He was a tiny man with a lion's voice.

"How you doing? I am Roger Allen Jones, New American Poet. Lamont Steptoe introduced me to you. I sell used books at the university." Roger was faithful to his sidewalk vendor business that, in conjunction with his own poetry, made him something of a Philadelphia celebrity.

"I'm alright," I said, smiling. "How you doin?"

"I'm alright, "he said with a hacking cough. "I liked your first book Water Song. You write any poetry lately?"

Roger lived for poetry like no one I have ever known. A native of West Philadelphia, he had been to Paris while serving in the Air Force but had never been to places near Philly, such as Cape May. Still, poetry was his passport to interiors and exteriors.

"Have you written your deathbed poems?"

I was stunned, but said I had not thought of it.

"Oh!" he said in his characteristic way, exhaling like a lion.

Roger had lots of time as he was semi-retired, so we started hanging out in the city's literary spots. We went to Chimes and hung out with Penn students. Time passed. Spring became summer again. I had been in the Treehouse for one year. After a trip to Boston to give a reading, I noticed I was having trouble breathing. One evening I developed a craving for cheese cake and decided to walk the three blocks to the grocery store that was also a writer's rendezvous. The three blocks took forever, and I felt like my torso was turning into cement. That night I tried to sleep but could not breathe unless I sat propped up with pillows. In an instant I remembered how my mother died of congestive heart failure following a heart attack, but I had never had a heart attack and so decided this was just a bad cold. It was Saturday night. The following morning I told Roger I was going to take a taxi to the emergency room to see about this cold.

My blood pressure was off the charts and my heart was in congestive failure. The nurse was adamant. "Get in that wheelchair. You are not going anywhere."

Hearts are supposed to be forever, like love, like the way I felt when my first love pressed up against me, the smell of her hair in my nose, her breath mine, two hearts beating together, and in my naïve adolescent way of seeing, two beating as one.

Hearts are the beautiful and petite things God holds in his hands before gently placing them inside us, and mine was now failing. My arteries were all clear, but my heart was swollen with heartache and the sadness of depression with which I had struggled for so long. There are secrets who know us when we do not know them. My heart held these secrets of the seeds of sadness.

I called family and friends, but the first person to see me was Roger. He came around the corner with a plastic grocery bag full of books and sat next to me in reverent silence, like someone gazing on a funeral shroud. All of us who knew and loved Roger knew that he drank, but he sat there sober and silent, asking now and then if there was anything I wanted. I could think of nothing. Barely able to walk but with no outward appearance of being ill, I looked out at the window, unable to grieve, thinking now and then of what it is to sleep, to sleep away, sleep away from knowing and consciousness into some kind of universal sameness, an original verse or maybe just nothing.

Prognoses are not like apples or Valentine's candy because prognoses often stink. Mine stank. I had five years to live taking seven medications and with limited mobility. After that I would need someone else's heart in order to live. At forty-three that meant I would not live to fifty without a transplant. Rumors of my death began to spread.

Did you hear? Michael S. Weaver died. Michael S. Weaver? Who was he? I heard he was hit by a car. No, that's not it. He was with some woman and had a heart attack. That's what I heard. He was from Baltimore. Really? How did he get to Brown? He did go to Brown, didn't he? Well, I heard he had some kind of disease.

No, it was cheese cake, and yet I live.

In elementary school we played the game of news gossip. The teacher would give one person in the room a fact which then traveled one by one throughout the class. The last person to receive it would tell the whole class the fact as he or she heard it. This final telling was always miles away from the original story. I wonder who buried me prematurely. I wonder who was quietly celebrating my move into the space of nothing. Literary friends are all too often less than genuine. People who really know and love you are sometimes the few who live outside the world of literary gamesmanship.

Home from the hospital, I arranged my various bottles of medicine on the end section of my futon bed so they looked like a small city. The large trees outside the window were a lovely canopy that helped me forget the gunfire that sometimes came   in the evening time. Roger and I would time our forays in the neighborhood so that we traveled in safer times, when the stickup artists were likely resting. The first week or so in any given month was usually safer due to the higher cash flow. Roger had to be admitted to Detox just after I came home from my one week stay at HUP. He was annoyed, of course.

He announced, "I asked the nurse if I should eat bananas."

"What did she say?"

"She said Mr. Jones, you need to eat a boatload of bananas."

"Roger, they can get you a new liver, like Mickey Mantle. You know they want to give me a new heart."

Roger would call my full name for emphasis or to subtly express the emotional fact of me having gotten on his last nerve.

"Michael S. Weaver. They will never make a Frankenstein out of me."

"That was the doctor, not the monster."

"Whatever. It's your life, Michael S. Weaver, your life. You live the way you want to live and die the way you want to die. I'm gonna die right up there in my apartment and be there for a week before they find me. That's how I'm going."

Hearts must have ears. I have no idea of what they look like, but hearts can hear us. With that faith I began talking to mine in an apologetic tone, vaguely hiding my sense of disappointment. It then occurred to me that perhaps my heart was fed up with me, with my stubborn determination, the long road of rocky relationships, pushing my body and mind beyond limits in the factories for fifteen years and now trying to break records for tenure at Rutgers. I didn't know who was angrier or who should be. More importantly, I still had a distance to go in firmly believing that the apple shaped loveliness that drove endless gallons of blood to where they were needed to go inside me was in fact as much me as I was it. I am my heart, and my heart is me. We are going out together.

When I took the catheterization test I had a chance to see my heart. Lying on the table in the tech room of the hospital, one of the doctors announced that my heart was visible on the screen. I peeped but was only able to bear it for three seconds. It was nothing like candy or apples or the candied apples we craved as children growing up in Baltimore. There was nothing as good as candied apples, although they could break your teeth. But this reality check was nothing like the dreams of the thing. I had worn out the thing that feeds my poetic being.

"Mr. Weaver, you have the heart of an old man."

Yeah right. I was born old.

I was given a list of things not to do, including driving for over thirty minutes at a time, so I immediately disobeyed, rented a new Ford Taurus and drove Roger to Cape May. It was his first time. We parked near the section of the beach near the old Christian Admiral Hotel. I walked slowly along, shooing seagulls. Roger just sat and studied the water. It was a clear and blue day, with an occasional dolphin spinning in the distance.

"How do you like it, Roger?"

"It sure beats watching television."

The doctors did not think exercise would help, but I returned to Taijiquan and the aspects of Chinese medicine it entails, especially cultivating the bioelectric Qi. As soon as I could take the train I went to Baltimore to see my old teacher, Shifu Huang Chien Liang. I had trained faithfully for six years, up until I left Baltimore to attend Brown's writing program. Entering academia, I fell away from regular practice, sometimes doing nothing for months at a time and then only practicing minimally. Roger was amused that I was doing gongfu and no amount of explanation would change his perception. It was all some attachment to a Bruce Lee machismo in Roger's way of seeing things.

We had an easier common language for machismo in westerns.

Roger was a tiny man with the voice of a behemoth "Hey Cisco! Let's go to the movies."

"Roger, I'm busy."

"Oh, I see. You doing your Taiji again. Well, call me when you get finished. That stuff won't help you. Better buy a good pistol."

"I'll call you when I finish."

"Okay, I'll be over here drinking."

Little by little I increased my exercise and range of walking, despite the doctor's warnings. Several other friends helped, including Ted and Emma, longtime friends from West Philadelphia. My cousins Curtis and Catherine were on standby, as they lived only a few minutes away, and the Butlers were always there. One night I had uncomfortable feelings in my chest, and I called downstairs to them at four-thirty in the morning. Mr. Butler came up and sat with me and convinced me to go to the emergency room, but there was nothing wrong. My heart was struggling to regain a normal rhythm.

One day the young cardiac resident who attended me called with good news. "Mr. Weaver, your heart has regained a normal rhythm."

A friend in California whom I knew only in cyberspace had taken care of her diabetic father with his congestive heart failure gave me supportive advice, including that she thought I had a much better chance than most with this affliction.

"For the rest of your life, it will be medicine, exercise, and heart appropriate eating. Accept that but do not accept all the doctors say. They don't know everything."

Roger's time was more limited than mine, and we both knew it, although we tried not to talk about. However, it was his will that failed before his organs. We went to lunch one day at a pizzeria restaurant around the corner on Baltimore Avenue, where I had a salad and ordered a roast beef sandwich for him. He would not eat.

He said, "I'm not happy anymore. But you listen to me. I want you to stop getting married all the time and settle down and enjoy your poetry and your teaching. You are the poet. Take care of your heart and let the women alone for awhile. When you get older good things will happen for you. But I'm done."

That fall we went to a benefit at Robin's bookstore. Larry Robin was struggling against Border's. Larry had been a friend of poets and writers for years and is a Philly cornerstone. We went down by bus as I do not own a car. We moved so slowly that after the bookstore event Teddy Harris helped us get onto the bus. I felt so old and worn and thanked Teddy for helping two old men get on the bus. He chuckled.

A year later, in the summer of ninety-six, I moved to Boston as I entered into a relationship with an Italian woman kind enough to encourage my exercise, especially the walking. Once during a trip to New York she encouraged me to walk from 125th Street to mid-Manhattan. I was wearing the prescription sunglasses I had to have as the Lasix made my eyes vulnerable to the sunlight. We walked for most of the afternoon. The relationship did not last, but she gave me the courage to walk a longer mile.

Roger would call and joke with us until he could no longer pay his phone bill. I left Boston to move to Lewisburg, Pennsylvania, and be poet-in-residence at Bucknell's Stadler Center for Poetry, where I called to check on him as often as possible.

It was the spring of ninety-seven, the year I took the name Afaa as given to me by Osunye Tess Onmueme. Afaa is Ibo for oracle.

Roger stopped answering the phone. I was worried and decided to go see him. It seemed he had been on the bus stop waiting to go buy a video player so he could watch his movies. Two stickup boys robbed him and pushed him around a little. I was distraught. A week later I came back. When I opened the door he was on the floor wrapped in a blanket, shivering. It was a warm day in May, a week or so before his birthday. He asked me to go get him some liquor.

"Roger, why don't you let me take you to the emergency room?"

"Why you want to do me that way? Can't you just do what I ask?"

It was not the liquor. He was asking to be granted his wish, to make his exit from this life in the way he often talked about, quietly in the space of his own home. I came back with a six pack of beer as the state stores were all closed. I could not get his cherished vodka. I used my keys again to open the door. He was still shaking.

"Thank you, Boss Hoss. You going back to the college now?"

I was choking. "Yeah, you know I'm teaching over there for a minute. Gotta pay these bills from the last marriage."

"You just remember what I told you about your poetry. Alright?"

"Roger, I'll be back in a few days."

Behind him was the darkness of the room, his face lit only by the candle. We went back to the language of the westerns.

He looked up and said, "I'll meet you at the pass."

I hung there in the silence for a minute. "Come on Roger."

"No, I'm done. Go on now."

"Meet you at the pass, partner."

When I came back the following weekend there was a towel at the door. A rod of fear went straight through me. I knew he was gone and the towel was there to cover the odor as he had not been found for several days. I knew all this but knocked on the door of a neighbor, who told me the same. I went in to say a goodbye in the space where we had talked about poetry, the death smell thick in the air. Roger was fifty-two.

African-Americans say an old black man is a miracle.

At fifty-three I am now one of Shifu Huang's Dao disciples. My health has gradually but steadily improved to where my heart functions normally with only two medications as opposed to the seven I was taking. Competing in martial arts competitions I have won gold, silver, and bronze medals. With help, I confronted the wounds of an abusive childhood and found the seeds of my sadness, the secret my heart had been holding, what it knew of me and kept until I could listen, even as the secrets took it into failure. Still I know I must live what one doctor described as a hygienic life.

In medical poetics my heart gave me what another doctor said was a limited insult. In other words it was a grave warning, all puns intended.

After convening an international conference on Chinese poetry in ninety-four, seven years after Roger died, I took a trip to China to meet some of the poets who attended my conference. I was in Hai Nan at a beach resort with Wang Xiaoni and her husband, speaking in Chinese about my motivations for holding the conference. As I explained that I wanted to give something back to the culture that gave so much to me, Wang Xiaoni, one of the most prominent poets in China, looked at me with deepest sincerity and said "Thank you."

Some vision formed itself in my eyes. On the beach I could see Roger sitting, gazing at the ocean, rocking a little the way he liked to rock with that lion's heart and voice that beat inside that tiny body.

"It sure beats watching television."

§

The art of Deborah Priestly

After Isaiah 10:19

*"And the remaining trees of his forests will be so few
that a child could write them down."*

If there were so few trees
A child could write them down,
No bears would climb for bees,
No wolf lie with the lamb.

If there were so few trees,
The rain that fell to ground
Would run away to seize
The land that grows the corn.

If there were so few trees
No shadow shade of brown
Would cool below the leaves
That sang the four winds' song.

If there were so few trees
Desert would come to sown,
And bony mountain's knees
Wear smooth under the sun.

If there were so few trees
The wrinkled earth must frown,
For there would never be
A child to write them down.

- Philip E. Burnham, Jr.

electronically manipulated photo found online by Steve Glines

"Ah, the Riviera!" Painting by Deborah M. Priestly (oil/sand)

Bagels with the Bards

The Bagelbards Anthology

No. 1

Edited by Molly Lynn Watt

So it came to pass that a couple of poets -- congenially munching their bagels in the spacious basement refectory of a bagelry called Finagle-a-Bagel on JFK in Harvard Square, all the while conjecturing upon the potential mental, spiritual and perhaps even physical salubriousness of occasional social interface with other human beings likewise blest or cused to pursue the word, to ply their craft or sullen art, in isolation -- gave birth to the idea of Bagelbards. At any rate, here it is: The First Annual Bagelbards Anthology, in celebration of the first full year of informal weekly Saturday morning gatherings of Bagelbards in the aforementioned spacius basement of Finagle-a-Bagel. Read it, and eat.

ISBN: 978-1-4116-8650-2
Paperback book $11.95
http://www.lulu.com/content/261048

"Still Life with Bagels," watercolor by Olga A. Moore, 2005

Bagels with the Bards

Bagelbard Anthology No. 2

Edited by Molly Lynn Watt
Introduction by Afaa Michael Weaver

It all came to fruition the day we made our first bagel, after a few energetic drafts of the thing. It got up from the table, shook its rolling shoulders, yawned from the hollow core mouth of itself, and began to dance. At that precise moment, the miracle came as sure as the Matrix Oracle would have predicted from over her pan of cookies. Sunlight hit the bagel, and it became lines on the floor, long lines that would have been perfect for any chorus line, but instead filled themselves with words, words that made promises to all of us. These words spoke the premise. The poet is a baker although he may never have the dough. We looked at each other and knew this was our creation myth, this dance of language on some piece of paper, or in our hearts, or in the burrowed brow of the manager trying to wrap his head around the idea that poets gather in the corner of his place on Saturdays and spend a few hours living, living, living. O bard, a bagel has become a poem.

ISBN: 978-1-4303-1654-1
Paperback book $16.95
http://www.lulu.com/content/729666

www.ingramcontent.com/pod-product-compliance
Lightning Source LLC
Chambersburg PA
CBHW030536030726
47495CB00004B/1019